CITY

The Black Coat Script Library

CITY

screenplay by
Randy & Jean-Marc Lofficier

inspired by the novel from
Joël Houssin

A Black Coat Press Book

Visit our website at www.blackcoatpress.com

ISBN 978-1-61227-084-5. First Printing. February 2012. Published by Black Coat Press, an imprint of Hollywood Comics.com, LLC, P.O. Box 17270, Encino, CA 91416.

Introduction

Joël Houssin (1953-) first came to our attention as an *enfant terrible* of French science fiction in the early 1970s. He was as talented and controversial as Harlan Ellison was in the U.S. His first book, *Locomotive Rictus* (1975), was a collection of three brilliant novellas; it was soon followed by a *Dangerous Visions*-like anthology, *Banlieues Rouges* [Red Suburbs] (1976), co-edited with Christian Vilà, which was a vibrant manifesto for French New Wave SF.

After that flamboyant start, Joël embarked on a series of science fiction novels for the famous "Anticipation" imprint of publisher Fleuve Noir, writing 11 novels in under five years. One of them, *Les Vautours* [The Vultures] (1985), about the politics of organ smuggling, won the prestigious Grand Prix de l'Imaginaire—an award which Joël won again in 1992 for his cyberpunk novel, *Le Temps du Twist*.

Two of Joël's "Anticipation" novels, *City* and *Game Over* (both 1983), made such a strong impression on us that we optioned the movie rights and adapted them into a single screenplay, originally entitled *Terminus Four*. After sending the screenplay to Joël, we awaited his feedback with some trepidation. We shouldn't have been worried, since his reaction was unadulterated enthusiasm and generous praise.

At the time, the Dino de Laurentiis organization was interested in the script, but they ran into their own problems, and eventually the project was shelved, as often happens in Hollywood.

Meanwhile, Joël went on to become one of France's best-selling thriller writers, having created the gangster saga of the "Dobermann" in 1981, which was made into a very stylish movie by director Jan Kounen in 1997. Today, Joël is one of French television's top show runners, having created such popular series as *Les Boeufs Carottes* (1995), *David Nolande* (2006) and *Eternelle* (2009), the last two incorporating genre elements.

In the intervening years, *Terminus Four*, later retitled *City* after the original novel, was resurrected twice, each time with real hope of emerging from development limbo. It underwent two complete rewrites, in part to update the political and technological aspects of the story. So the version that you are about to read is really version 3.2. In the process, we have strayed even further from the source material, to the extent that the script now is more "inspired" by Joël's novel than "based on," in the same way that *Twelve Monkeys* was inspired by Chris Marker's *La Jetée*.

Randy & Jean-Marc Lofficier

CITY

FADE IN:
Black screen.

A CHIRON BEGINS TO SCROLL ON SCREEN

> CHIRON
> When the international community of scientists started to warn the world of the dangers of Global Warming, some within the United States refused to listen.

> CHIRON
> Without the cooperation of America, all efforts to control Global Warming were a failure.

> CHIRON
> Most of Florida, Louisiana and parts of Texas disappeared under rising sea levels.

> CHIRON
> The secession movement whose seeds had been planted in 2009 caused the break-up of the United States.

> CHIRON
> "ATLANTA - 2089"

EXT. ATLANTA – DUSK
Atlanta is now fully visible on the screen. The skyline is familiar but changed. It is clear that the city is no longer what it once was. In 2089, Atlanta is a disaster area.

The sky is yellow with pollution. Garbage lies uncollected along the sidewalks. Insects breed in stagnant water and weed-like vegetation.

Wrecked automobile husks and abandoned machinery line the streets. The high-rises are dirty and filled with broken windows. Some buildings show traces of fire and explosions.

On a wall, we SEE the tattered remains of a poster showing a modified Georgia flag with the motto "Resurgens – Rising Again" still readable.

Even Atlanta's residents have started to devolve into strange, animalistic shapes. We SEE a misshapen, man-sized creature with rat-like features scurry out of a sewer entrance and disappear into the darkness.

CAMERA ZOOMS IN ON a red, heavily-armored SUV that slowly crawls through the streets. We recognize it immediately as a police vehicle. It is futuristic and threatening. We cannot see its occupant through the tinted windshield.

The SUV moves TOWARDS CAMERA. We SEE a sign on the door that reads: "ATLANTA - POLICE."

<u>INT. POLICE SUV – DUSK</u>
CLOSE UP ON a pair of hands encased in thick, black gloves that are almost caressing the steering wheel.

CAMERA PULLS BACK to reveal PATRICK STAN-TON. He is in his late thirties; tall and attractive in a tough, cynical sort of way.

He fell into being a cop out of an idealistic desire to help people, but cynicism has long taken over. Still, he's good at his job and he knows it. He has been working in Atlanta for over ten years and his face reflects his weariness and the death of his illusions.

A CRACKLING, BEEPING sound breaks the silence. It comes from a computer embedded in the dashboard.
The face of a weasely-looking man appears on the screen. His name is MOREL.

> MOREL
> Officer Stanton. Officer Stanton. Report, Officer Stanton.

Stanton ignores the call and remains motionless, lost in his own reveries.

> MOREL
> Stanton! You asshole! Come in now or I'll send a drone after you.

Stanton touches the screen.

> STANTON
> Fuck you, Morel! I'm on my break. Go to Hell.

> MOREL
> Screw your fucking break, Stanton! We just got an A-1 call near your position. A Normal named Willman is stuck on Block 12 in Cabbagetown. Go get him out.

                    STANTON
Cabbagetown? That's Iguana territory. What's a
fucking Normal doing there?

                    MOREL
That's not your problem. Get him out, or you'll
be patrolling OTP before you take your next
piss. That's a promise. Later.

                    STANTON
Up yours.
            (he shuts off his screen)
Shitface.

EXT. ATLANTA – NIGHT
The SUV revs up and takes off in a burst of speed.

It reaches a freeway on-ramp marked "INTERSTATE
NORTH." A sign blinks out "CURFEW" non-stop, spil-
ling bright, garish red light onto its surroundings.

INT. SUV – NIGHT
Stanton drives onto the Interstate.

With one hand, he hits various spots reading "DEFENSE
SYSTEMS" and "ATTACK SYSTEMS." on a touch
screen setting them into "lethal mode."

From the dashboard unit comes a message: "CURFEW!
ANY CITIZENS STILL IN TRANSIT MUST NOW
BROADCAST THEIR EMERGENCY IDENTIFICA-
TION NUMBERS. CURFEW!"

Stanton switches off the unit.

<u>EXT. INTERSTATE – NIGHT</u>
Stanton's car zooms down the Interstate. He passes a black motorcycle that is stopped on the side of the road.

This is DEATH. Death is dressed in black skin-tight leathers. His face is completely covered by a red helmet with a skull design. In the dark orb of the eyes, we SEE two glowing, green points. Soon, Death's secret identity will be revealed.

A small CREATURE that looks like a gelatinous, translucent rat comes crawling to Death's hands. He strokes it distractedly.

Death addresses the creature. His voice is soft and purring, yet deadly.

> DEATH
> Look, angel... A police officer... Alone after curfew...
>> (a pause)
> You have a date with Death, Cop...

Death's powerful bike ROARS to life.

The bike and its grim passenger zoom onto the Interstate.

<u>INT. STANTON'S SUV – NIGHT</u>
STANTON'S P.O.V.: A dot in the rearview mirror grows rapidly.

Stanton recognizes Death on his bike.

STANTON

Oh, shit!

EXT. INTERSTATE – NIGHT
CLOSE UP on Death, his green eyes GLOWING inside his helmet.

The space between the two opponents closes. Death speaks with an amplified voice.

DEATH
Hey, Cop, why are you in such a rush?

INT. STANTON'S SUV – NIGHT
STANTON
I don't have time for this kind of shit now.

He touches a spot on his screen marked TURBO so it goes to "MAX."

EXT. INTERSTATE – NIGHT
The vehicle literally jumps ahead. Rubber burns as he takes a sharp curve, almost at the outer edge of the Inter-state.

Death also accelerates.

Stanton is faster, but Death is more nimble. He cuts the curve, which brings him on a course parallel with the SUV's.

He makes a gesture with his hand as if he is throwing something at the SUV.

A couple of his "pets" jump from his extended arm onto Stanton's car.

Where the "pets" bite the car, acid from their jaws attacks the metal.

INT. STANTON'S SUV – NIGHT
All the warning lights are blinking red.

A "pet" is gnawing at the windshield.

Suddenly, there's a loud THUMPING sound.

Stanton swerves. He looks pissed.

EXT. INTERSTATE – NIGHT
Death is using a whirling mace to SMASH the side of the SUV.

DEATH
Don't fight it, Cop. Death can be sweet.

INT. STANTON'S SUV – NIGHT
STANTON
(shouting)
Fuck you!

He swerves again to avoid the next blow.

He then touches places on the "ATTACK SYSTEMS" panel.

EXT. INTERSTATE – NIGHT
Stanton's car is suddenly engulfed in fire.

Death's "pets" burn and drop off with SCREECHING noises.

Death himself disappears in a huge fireball.

INT. STANTON'S SUV – NIGHT
The windshield has become dark red. The temperature in the car rises.

The gas gauge is going down slowly, but steadily, TO-WARDS ZERO.

Stanton stops the fireball. The indicator stops, fairly close to zero but not quite there.

EXT. INTERSTATE – NIGHT
The flames linger for a minute, but the rushing speed of the car extinguishes them.

Death is nowhere to be seen.

INT. STANTON'S SUV – NIGHT
Stanton slows down. He scrutinizes the rearview mirror, looking for signs of his opponent. There are none.

He then turns to look ahead.

There is a deep crack on the windshield where one of Death's "pets" has attacked the glass.

Suddenly, the whirling mace of Death strikes the very same spot, causing the windshield to EXPLODE in a thousand, flying particles.

EXT. INTERSTATE – NIGHT
Death materializes from the left side of the car. He pre-pares to strike again.

DEATH
You can't fight Death, Cop. Death is forever.

INT. STANTON'S SUV – NIGHT
Stanton clears fragments of glass from his hair.

STANTON
Shit! Shit! Shit!

He swerves to avoid another blow. Then, he piles on the brakes.

STANTON
Go fuck yourself, Death!

EXT. INTERSTATE – NIGHT
Stanton's car spins wildly. Tires SCREECHING, it ends up facing the opposite direction.

Death accelerates out of the way, to avoid being crushed. He then slows down.

Stanton has taken this opportunity to zoom off in the direction from which he came.

Death stops his bike and watches the police SUV disap-pear.

DEATH

Not bad, Cop. You're a worthy opponent for Death...

INT. STANTON'S SUV – NIGHT

Stanton is sweating, shaking and out of breath. After a second, he touches the communication area on his control screen.

STANTON

Get me Morel.

There's a brief pause, then Morel appears on the screen. He looks annoyed.

MOREL

Why aren't you doing your job, Stanton? If the Guanas kill that citizen...

STANTON

Stuff it, Morel! I just had a little visit from Death! My rig's trashed; you're gonna have to send Baracca to Cabbagetown and I'm going to limp back to HQ.

MOREL

Damn it, Stanton! What the hell did you want piss around with him for? That's the third cruiser he's wrecked this week. Where am I gonna get the budget for this?

STANTON

Not my problem, asshole. Stanton out.

INT. STANTON'S SUV – NIGHT
Stanton turns off his com screen and sighs. He starts driving, slowly.

EXT. INTERSTATE – NIGHT
A DIFFERENT POLICE SUV is driving down the Inter-state.

This SUV is decorated with dozens of colorful decals depicting good luck symbols. The muffled sound of MIDDLE-EASTERN MUSIC is heard over the passage of the car.

The driver is an exotic Middle-Eastern woman. Her name is BARACCA. Her voice is deep and sexy, with a slight Iraqi accent.

Baracca is in her early thirties. She is the daughter of an American GI and an Iraqi woman. Her GI father was able to bring her and her mother to America when she was still young enough to think that the streets were paved with gold. Her experiences since moving have left her disappointed with that dream. Her Iraqi mother gave her a deeply superstitious nature; her GI father taught her how to stand up for herself. The poverty of her early childhood left her with an overwhelming sense of greed and fear of not having "enough," whatever that means. Although she looks very sensual, she is hard as nails and all business.

Unlike Stanton's car, which is clean and impersonal, Baracca's is filled with mysterious objects and trinkets. Her com screen lights up and we SEE Morel's face yet again.

MOREL

Hey, Baracca, what's that crap I hear in the background?

BARACCA

Stop bustin' my balls, Morel. You can't tell me what to listen to in my rig!

MOREL

We don't have time for this shit again. I need you to go clean up a mess that Stanton left me.
(he pauses)
There's a Normal stuck in Cabbagetown under attack by the Guanas. You need to go get him out.

BARACCA

That's not my job. Why can't Stanton do it?

MOREL

He decided to do a little dance with Death instead and now he's torn up his rig. So, just do it, 'kay?

BARACCA
(turning off her com screen)
Shit!

EXT. INTERSTATE – NIGHT
Baracca's SUV puts on its flashing lights and roars down the Interstate.

EXT. BARACCA'S SUV – NIGHT
The SUV exits the Interstate. It enters into an area that once may have been an attractive, residential section filled with condos, etc. It has now fallen into the same decayed state as the rest of City.

The streets are completely deserted. An occasional SCREAM (human or animal?) cuts through the SILENCE of the night. The SUV slows down.

INT. BARACCA'S SUV – NIGHT
Baracca looks at a small GPS map screen where a red man-shaped BLIP has appeared.

EXT. ATLANTA – NIGHT
The SUV accelerates again, now appearing to be headed in a definite direction. The outside SILENCE is suddenly broken by the WAIL of the SUV's powerful SIREN.

EXT. BLOCK 12 – NIGHT
Another car, a green compact, is being assaulted by a mob. They throw rubble at it, and try to break inside.

The PASSENGER inside the car looks terrified. He is a pudgy, small man in a cheap suit.

The MEMBERS OF THE CROWD are not quite normal. Their skin is slightly greenish and is peeling in places. They all wear dark glasses. Their movements, although strong, seem slower than what you would expect from a regular human.

Baracca's SUV comes around the Block's corner, siren BLARING.

INT. BARACCA'S SUV – NIGHT
Baracca sees that the mob is attacking the other car.
She hits various places on the touch screen.

EXT. BLOCK 12 – NIGHT
Baracca's car stops with a SQUEALING of its brakes.
The policewoman's voice comes out of a hidden louds-
peaker.

> BARACCA (O.S.)
> This is Officer Baracca! Fun's over, kiddies. Go
> home before someone gets hurt. This is your on-
> ly warning.

One of the strange kids throws a metal can at the SUV.

INT. BARACCA'S SUV – NIGHT
There is a loud CLANK as the can hits the car.

> BARACCA
> Shit!

Her hand automatically glides to another touch screen
position.

EXT. BLOCK 12 – NIGHT
A HISS of green mace gas spurts out of the SUV. A few
attackers back off.

> BARACCA (O.S.)
> If you shitheads give me any more trouble, I'm
> going to splatter you all over the fucking street.

A loud, threatening, WHIRRING noise comes out of the SUV. Several vicious-looking weapons emerge from panels in the car's body. The lights switch from their normal beam to an ominous reddish light.

The faces of the attackers show fear. They look at each other as if sending a silent message.

Suddenly, they split up and run away. In a second, the street is deserted.

EXT. BLOCK 12 – NIGHT
The two cars are now facing each other.

INT. BARACCA'S SUV – NIGHT
The face and voice of WILLMAN, the small man in the green car, come out of the com unit. His voice sounds whiney and grating. It is extremely irritating.

> WILLMAN
> Thank you, Officer. I don't know why those crit-
> ters attacked me...

> BARACCA
> (suspicious)
> Guanas are usually pretty harmless. They're le-
> thargic most of the time. They only come out at
> night... What were you doing around here?

> WILLMAN
> (embarrassed)
> Well... I... I just was passing through...

Baracca laughs sarcastically.

> BARACCA
> Passing through Cabbagetown? Hey, Normal,
> I'm a woman, not stupid! Nobody "passes
> through" Cabbagetown anymore... Unless you
> wanted to have some fun with a Guana girl, isn't
> that it? Heard all the stories... figured it was safe
> enough during the day... and then you got stuck
> here.

> WILLMAN
> I haven't done anything illegal. I've gotta go
> now.

<u>EXT. BLOCK 12 – NIGHT</u>
There are engine noises. Willman's car SPUTTERS, but
refuses to start.

Baracca's voice comes over the loudspeaker.

> BARACCA (O.S.)
> Bet you had some fun too. Except the Guana's
> brothers didn't like it.
>   (her tone hardens)
> What's your I.D., Citizen?

<u>INT. WILLMAN'S CAR – NIGHT</u>
The fat, little man is shifting uncomfortably. He tries to
start his car several times. Unsuccessfully.

> WILLMAN
> Electro-repairman Willman, Second Class. I.D.
> number, 4789-DZ-8003.

WILLMAN (cont'd)
(pleading)
You have to help me, Officer! The critters must
have damaged my car...

INT. BARACCA'S SUV – NIGHT
BARACCA
They're not "critters," scum. They're Genetic
Anomalies...
(a pause)
Electro-repairman... You're on strike, aren't
you, Citizen?

There is a long silence.

WILLMAN (O.S.)
Er... Yeah, we are, but...

BARACCA
(starting her car)
Well, then, that's it. Nice meeting you, repair-
man.

WILLMAN (O.S.)
(genuinely alarmed)
Hey, wait! You can't just leave me here. You've
got to help me. You're a Cop. It's your duty to
take me home...
(a pause)
I have your badge number. I can report you. You
have to take me home.

EXT. BLOCK 12 – NIGHT
Baracca's car goes around Willman's and drives away.

INT. BARACCA'S SUV – NIGHT

Baracca smiles; it's a wicked smile. She's enjoying herself.

> BARACCA
>
> You're wrong, Citizen. My duty was to clear
> away the mob. I've done that. I don't have to
> take you home...
>> (a pause)
>
> My waste disposal unit has been shot for two
> months now, and I can't get it fixed... So, why
> don't you do as I do, repairman. Be patient. En-
> joy.

EXT. BLOCK 12 – NIGHT

Willman's car sits motionless.

> WILLMAN (O.S.)
>
> Please, Officer! Please! Take me home. Don't
> leave me here. They'll come back. I'll fix your
> waste disposal unit. Right now, if you want.

INT. BARACCA'S SUV – NIGHT

Through the back window, Willman's car fades into the
distance.

> BARACCA
>
> Well, well... Working when your union is on
> strike... That's against the law, Citizen! But
> don't worry. I won't say a word. Later!

Baracca flicks the com unit off.

BARACCA

Shitface.

She inhales on the end of a long, brown, opiate cigarette, and lets the smoke slowly escape from her mouth.

BARACCA
(to herself)
So, the Big Man played with Death. I don't like it; there's trouble coming for us...

EXT. POLICE HQ – DAWN
Stanton's battered SUV barely limps into the parking lot. A few seconds later, Baracca's truck squeals into the lot. It parks right next to Stanton.

Baracca and Stanton get out of their cars and walk towards each other.

BARACCA
Thanks for nothing, Big Man!

STANTON
Eat it, Baracca. It's not like I had much choice. Death came after me out on the Interstate.

BARACCA
Why do you want to mess with that nutbag, anyway? He's out to get any Cop he can.

STANTON
Didn't you hear what I said? He came after me! 'Sides, I know how much you love hanging out in Cabbagetown!

BARACCA

The Guanas are better looking than you are and
probably better in bed too!

She breaks into a sensual laugh. Stanton too starts to
laugh.

STANTON

Fuck you, Baracca! I'm too tired to have this
conversation. I'm gonna get a new rig and then
I'm outta here.

The two turn to go in different directions, Baracca heading inside the building and Stantion heading off to the
garage. Before she goes inside, Baracca turns and rushes
back to Stanton.

BARACCA

I'm not teasing now, Big Man. The word is out
on the street -- Death is on a rampage. Don't
think it's a game; Death isn't human. He isn't
like the other critters either... He comes out of
nowhere and kills, just for the joy of it. He's an
evil djinn, like the ones that come from the
desert and take my people in the night...
            (a beat, then seriously)
He scares me. Bad.

STANTON

You're right about one thing; he's not just any
old street banger. He's fucking insane. But, he
doesn't scare me.

Stanton again heads for the garage but turns his head to yell over his shoulder at Baracca.

STANTON
Thanks for the head's up anyway. Later!

INT. GARAGE – DAWN
Stanton is in a vast garage, signing his car in for repairs. The SUV is in sorry shape. Its paint is burned; there are dents where Death's mace struck it, and where the "pets" have chewed the metal.

A YOUNG MECHANIC walks around the car, taking notes on a tablet computer.

MECHANIC
Stanton?

STANTON
Yeah?

MECHANIC
(looking up)
What happened?

STANTON
(cool)
A little argument with Death.

The Mechanic whistles. He looks at the car, then shakes his head. He hands the tablet to Stanton.

MECHANIC
Sign here.

Stanton scribbles something.

> MECHANIC
> I'll have another car ready for you in an hour.

Stanton starts to leave. The Mechanic calls out to him.

> MECHANIC
> You're one lucky bastard!

> STANTON
> (without turning)
> Ain't got nothing to do with luck, kid.

EXT. ATLANTA – CASTLEBERRY HILL – DAWN
Day is breaking over the renovated warehouses and lofts of Castleberry Hill. The Hill is better maintained than other parts of ATLANTA. Castleberry Hill is where people that cannot afford the prices of the SoNo live.

In the b.g., is the classier, richer, corporate zone of So-No, with its futuristic towers adorned with corporate logos: "BLACKSPEAR," "U.F.G.," "MIKRATEK," etc...

(There are many big corporations in Atlanta, but using or not using them can be worked out at a later date).

Stanton's SUV is approaching a renovated warehouse.

EXT. WAREHOUSE – DAWN
Stanton's car stops in front of a reinforced steel gate.

INT. STANTON'S CAR – DAWN
Stanton's gloved hands quickly punch a series of figures on his panel. The code plays a musical phrase.

A pause. Then, an obviously pre-recorded message comes over the com unit.

MESSAGE
IDENTIFICATION   ACKNOWLEDGED.
PLEASE WAIT.

EXT. WAREHOUSE – DAWN
Stanton's car idles NOISILY for a couple of seconds.

Then, the steel gate slides open with a GRATING sound. There is a second steel gate inside. The SUV drives into the building.

The outer gate starts closing behind it.

INT. WAREHOUSE GARAGE – DAWN
The garage is dark and totally deserted. Stanton's body language, however, expresses watchful caution as he walks towards an elevator.

The elevator doors slide open.

INT. ELEVATOR – DAY
Stanton steps in and punches in another series of figures. The elevator shakes a little, then moves upward.

INT. KOREY'S LOFT – DAY
The doorbell CHIMES. KOREY goes to the door. She is a very attractive black woman, in her late twenties or

mid-thirties. She works as an administrative assistant at BlackSpear. She looks very modern and fashionable. Her movements, however, are slightly lethargic.

Her face is drawn, and she has bags under her eyes. She has the aura of someone who is seriously hooked on drugs.

Stanton's voice can be heard through the door.

> STANTON (O.S.)
> It's me.

Korey opens the door. She sounds slightly irritated at Stanton.

> KOREY
> I'm not alone.

Stanton dumps his helmet on the floor, but keeps his gloves on.

> STANTON
> (annoyed)
> Who is he?

> KOREY
> (lowering her voice)
> His name is Orloff. He brought me home. He wanted to leave, but I insisted that he stay.
> (more acerbically)
> You know what it's like around here. You wouldn't want him to get killed, just because you were coming over, would you?

STANTON
You didn't answer my question -- who is he?

KOREY
He's high up at BlackSpear. Come in; I'll intro-
duce you. You can't stand out there forever.

Stanton follows Korey into her living room. The room is
sparsely decorated, with a couch, a coffee table, and a
few pieces of plastic furniture. Scattered around are
transparent jars filled with colorful pills.

One wall of the room is made up of an enormous flat
panel TV screen. In front are two standing "chairs"
equipped with arm rests, foot pads and head rests with
"arms" that circle the user's head when they are in the
chair. They lean at a slight angle, so that when you are in
one, you aren't completely upright. This is a futuristic
"holo-game" device that can be used by one or two players. Although we see the image on the flat panel, when
someone is playing, they feel as if they are physically
inside the game.

The screen is freeze-framed on a very beautiful, black-
haired girl with the title "LUNA" artistically rendered
beneath. In the corner of the screen is the logo of Black-
Spear Holdings, the company that makes the game. The
logo is a black circle with a diagonal white line running
through it.

ORLOFF sits on the couch. He is tall, lean and very
carefully groomed. He looks like a typical, bland execu-

tive, dressed in a conservative suit, but he could easily be very frightening if he became angry.

He stands up as Stanton enters the room.

>   ORLOFF
>   You must be Patrick. I'm glad to meet you. Ko-
>   rey has told me a lot about you.

>   STANTON
>   She has, huh?

>   ORLOFF
>   Yes, Officer Stanton. I've always admired At-
>   lanta's police force. It must be a fascinating line
>   of work... The excitement. The danger.

Stanton ignores the remark and slumps into a chair. Korey tries to rescue the situation.

>   KOREY
>   (to Stanton)
>   You don't look too great. You want me to get
>   you something...

Stanton nods.

Korey grabs a jar and starts pulling out blue and white capsules.

>   KOREY
>   Three?

Stanton nods again.

Korey pours a glass of something, and drops the capsules in it. While they dissolve, she makes conversation.

> KOREY
> Orloff is one of BlackSpear's top holo designers...
> > (pointing at the big screen)
> He designed Moon Quest. It's really deviant. It's my favorite.

Stanton grabs the cocktail and downs it in one gulp. He still remains silent.

There is a painfully long pause. Then, Korey turns towards Orloff, embarrassed.

> KOREY
> Please excuse Patrick, Orloff. He's like this sometimes when he gets off shift. He'll be better when the "grannies" start to work.

She changes the subject, to something that is obviously important to her.

> KOREY
> > (still talking to Orloff)
> Tell me about Luna. What's she really like? I've been riding the chair non-stop since I've had it.

> ORLOFF
> Well, she's actually quite a charming young woman. Her game has been the most popular of all our products. There are already over 20 million in circulation.

KOREY

It's so deviant! When I plug into it, it's like I'm really her... I like it best when she battles the Silica Worms for possession of the Rook Mountains.

ORLOFF
(smiling smugly)
I must admit, that is one of my best ideas...

Stanton has now relaxed under the influence of the "grannies." He interrupts the conversation.

STANTON
Holo bullshit!

Korey turns angrily towards him, starting to snap at him.

KOREY
Patrick! You have no right...

Orloff silences her with a commanding gesture which seems slightly out of character.

ORLOFF
Please, Korey. I'd like to hear what your friend has to say.

STANTON
Your fucking holo-games are a load of shit. My ex spent her whole waking life inside one. In the end, the guys in the white suits had to drag her away to force feed her. Her brain was fucking mush by the time they unplugged her...

ORLOFF

Hmm, yes... That was a problem with the old models... But, our new holo-games, like "Moon Quest"...

(pointing at the screen)

...take care of that. The chairs are programmed to stop if they sense that you haven't met your minimum daily nutritional requirements.

Stanton is now more awake. He straightens up in his chair.

STANTON

I'll tell you what your holo-games do... They make my job a fucking nightmare, that's what.

ORLOFF

I'm afraid I don't quite follow you.

Stanton's anger keeps growing.

STANTON

Because of your fucking holo-games, everybody is paranoid as hell about those poor critters out there. It's the Silica Worms, the Moon Monster... What's next? The Giant Turnip? People can't tell what's real anymore.

ORLOFF

(with a sly smile)

They're harmless entertainment. We give the people what they want, that's all. Nobody forces anybody to buy one of our games.

ORLOFF (cont'd)
(more aggressively)
What are you afraid of, Patrick?

STANTON
Afraid?

ORLOFF
(becoming excited)
Yes. I mean, what is it that you fear most when you're out there alone in the city? Every man is afraid of something... or someone.

Korey swallows a couple of purple capsules.

KOREY
Patrick isn't afraid of anything.

ORLOFF
(with a strange look in his eyes)
Is that true?

STANTON
I'm paid to protect the Citizens when they're afraid. Not to be afraid myself.

ORLOFF
All the same, you must face terrible horrors each time you go out there... We hear reports of newer, more dangerous mutations every day.

STANTON
If that's how you feel, why the fuck do you set foot outside your door to go to work?

Orloff gives a polite laugh.

> ORLOFF
> I don't need to set foot outside my door. I
> brought Korey home, but that's an exception.
> Like more and more of our personnel, I live in-
> side BlackSpear Tower.
> > (a pause)
> We're at the forefront of a new era. In a few
> years, Atlanta's streets will become a no-man's
> land, left entirely to the critters. The elite will
> work and live inside the towers.

Stanton has listened to Orloff's speech with a growing
look of distaste.

> STANTON
> You fucking make me sick!

Korey is jolted out of her trance. Stanton's vehement
outburst frightens her.

> KOREY
> Patrick! Stop it!

Stanton ignores her. He stares at Orloff, disgust in his
eyes.

> STANTON
> You've got no idea what Atlanta's really like.
> This place was meant to be a cultural beacon,
> not a fucking concentration camp. It's bastards
> like you that made it what it is today...

KOREY

Patrick! Orloff is my guest!

Orloff makes a placating gesture.

ORLOFF

It's all right, Korey. I think Patrick is getting carried away...

STANTON

(unstoppable)

You talk about critters. Let me tell you about critters. Lots of them are better than the soulless parasites that live inside your towers...

ORLOFF

Hum...

KOREY

You don't have to let him talk to you that way...

Stanton explodes, and begins to scream at Korey.

STANTON

What's going on here? You let any asshole walk into your apartment? You fucking him too?

ORLOFF

I think it's time I left.

STANTON

Fine! Get out! Tell the fucking elite in those towers of shit, that outside there's still a world full of human beings.

Orloff gets up.

Korey screams at Stanton.

> KOREY
> Patrick! I forbid you to...

> STANTON
> You forbid me to what?

She turns towards Orloff, who has put on his coat.

> KOREY
> You don't have to leave. You don't need to lis-
> ten to this pig's...

Orloff stops her in a brutally authoritative way, which
reveals a previously unseen facet of his character.

> ORLOFF
> Silence, Korey!

She shuts up instantly, and staggers backward. Orloff
walks towards the door. We HEAR the NOISE of the
security systems being switched on and off.

Korey then turns towards Stanton.

> KOREY
> Well, great! Why are you doing this to me? You
> want to get me fired? You don't have any right
> to talk to me like that. You don't own me. I'm
> not your ex...

                    STANTON
          That guy gives me the creeps.

Korey LAUGHS bitterly.

                    KOREY
          He gives YOU the creeps? Have you looked at
          yourself lately? You couldn't even stand up
          straight when you came in, and you still haven't
          taken off your gloves. You think that's Normal
          behavior?

Stanton removes his boots, which fall LOUDLY to the
floor.

                    STANTON
          I don't like to take off my gloves. You should
          know that by now. I'm tired. I want to go to bed.

He walks towards the bedroom.

INT. BEDROOM – DAY
A digital clock on a nightstand reads 10:00 a.m.

Stanton is lying on his side in bed, under a sheet. His
hands are in view, showing that he has not removed his
gloves.

Korey walks into the room from the living room. She is
wearing an attractive kimono. She stands there for several seconds, silently watching Stanton as he sleeps.

She then drops the kimono and goes to lay down by his
side.

Her light brown hand caresses his back, starting at the shoulder and moving downwards, until it disappears under the sheet.

Stanton's eyes open, and he turns over to face her.

EXT. BLACKSPEAR TOWER – EVENING
The sun is just starting to set over City. The warm colors of evening soften the uglier signs of decay.

INT. BLACKSPEAR COMPUTER BANKS – EVENING
Data is streaming quickly across a monitor screen.

The picture FREEZES on "ATLANTA POLICE EVALUATION / SECURITY RATINGS."

Names SCROLL on the screen. The scrolling stops and the screen reads: "PATRICK G. STANTON - EFFICIENCY RATING : 94.76" "ALEXANDRIA N. BARACCA - EFFICIENCY RATING : 94.74"

BlackSpear's logo fills the screen.

Orloff is sitting in front of the monitor. He looks up and into space, and then smiles.

ORLOFF
Perfect. They'll be perfect.

He laughs a slightly maniacal and unnerving laugh.

On another screen is Luna looking beautiful and enigmatic, almost as if she is lit up from inside.

EXT. PRESIDENTIAL TOWER – NIGHT
The Presidential Tower is a massive building, decorated with patriotic paintings, fountains, etc... It is mostly dark, except for a lit penthouse.

On closer examination of the building, it's obvious that the paintings have been disfigured by graffiti, and that garbage is floating in the fountains.

The large, penthouse windows are lit up.

INT. PRESIDENTIAL PENTHOUSE – NIGHT
PRESIDENT ASTASI BRAUNSBERG is watching an X-rated show on a giant flat panel wall screen.

He is of indeterminate race and is a truly enormous man. Although big, he does not look fat. He is, in fact, built more like a sumo wrestler. Braunsberg is dressed in a colorful kimono, and is sitting in a heap of silk cushions. He occasionally picks raw tuna out of a silver bowl, and slurps it down noisily.

TWO VERY YOUNG GIRLS in scanty clothes lay at his feet on the thickly-carpeted floor. One is scratching the head of a pet leopard.

A bell rings; then a voice comes out of a hidden loudspeaker.

VOICE
Security Chief Boone, Mister President.

BRAUNSBERG

Let him in.

Somewhere a door has opens and closes with a SWISH-
ING sound.

MITCHELL ("CRAZY MITCH") BOONE walks into
the room. He is a tall, gaunt, older man with white hair
and cold, blue eyes. He looks very strict, almost uncom-
promising, in his immaculate police uniform. There is
something of the fanatic about him.

BRAUNSBERG
(still watching the show)
What's wrong now, Boone? Are you having
more problems with my people?

BOONE
(hostile)
I always have problems with your people, Mister
President.

Braunsberg noisily slurps down another bit of tuna.
Boone looks away, faintly disgusted.

Braunsberg switches off the television. He turns to face
Boone.

BRAUNSBERG
You know your problem, Boone? I'll tell you
your problem. It's you. You're the problem.
You're cold, like a machine... I don't like ma-
chines, and neither do my people...

BRAUNSBERG (cont'd)

Never forget that, here you're among the privi-
leged. You could be out there, living with the
critters...

He points out the window and laughs sarcastically.

BRAUNSBERG

The great citizens of my beautiful city... Ha!
          (more serious)
Instead, every day you walk in the gardens of
Marietta Street. You live in a top-security high
rise in SoNo. Your position gives you the power
to do almost anything you want...
          (shouting)
So, why the fuck don't you enjoy it, instead of
always looking like you've got hemorrhoids?

A pause. Boone ignores the presidential outburst. His
confidence does not appear shaken as he calmly continues.

BOONE

The new V.P. of Mikratek has requested an
emergency meeting with you, Mister President.
Tonight.

Braunsberg explodes. He throws the tuna bowl across
the room.

The two girls scurry away and huddle together in a corner.

The leopard opens one eye, surveys the scene, then apparently goes back into its sleepy trance.

                    BRAUNSBERG
                    (angry)
Shit! What the fuck does he want?

Boone answers calmly, as if he were reasoning with a child.

                    BOONE
The elections are coming. We've learned that...

                    BRAUNSBERG
                    (eyes narrowing)
We? Who's we?

Boone loses his composure for a fraction of a second. But he quickly recomposes himself.

                    BOONE
                    (stressing the first word)
Mikratek has learned that the Opposition is planning to concentrate its attack on urban violence; especially in Atlanta. They intend to focus their whole campaign on what's happening here. The violence in the streets, the high incidence of genetic anomalies...

                    BRAUNSBERG
                    (angrily)
That's a load of shit! Nobody in the country cares about what's happening in Atlanta... Nobody except you.

BOONE

Don't underestimate the threat, Mister President. There are powerful interests invested in Atlanta. Mikratek, BlackSpear, U.F.G., they all want to protect their investments. They know the Opposition intends to nationalize their assets, so they're behind you...

(a pause)

For now... Frankly, your management has been less than successful. Atlanta is running a billion dollar deficit and...

Braunsberg slurps another piece of tuna.

BRAUNSBERG

So, what's new? Atlanta has run a deficit for decades. She's like a woman, nothing's too expensive for her.

BOONE

(sarcastic)

More like a whore, you mean, an old whore... Look around you, Mister President. Atlanta attracts only parasites. Every year, the forest takes back another meter or two. Foreign capital is afraid to invest. There hasn't been any new construction in five years. The quality of life has become not only dangerous, but unhealthy. A lot of people have already left, and more are leaving every day...

(more heatedly)

We've reached a critical point, we have to do something.

BRAUNSBERG

Don't shout at me! I'm still the President! Besides, you're upsetting Aga. He doesn't like shouting. Do you, my pet?

Braunsberg pets the leopard, which is now fully awake and angry looking.

Boone looks at Braunsberg with something akin to hate in his eyes.

BOONE

You really don't care about the city, do you?

BRAUNSBERG
(shrugging)
The problems aren't my fault. I've inherited the mess.

Boone makes a small, sarcastic laugh.

BOONE

Ha! I know how you became President. You didn't inherit anything, you...

Braunsberg jumps off of the cushions with a speed that belies his mass. He looks furious. He opens and closes his enormous, knotted hands.

BRAUNSBERG

Enough! I can break you in half without even trying, Boone...

Boone backs away and makes a pacifying gesture.

                    BOONE
        Okay, okay! I'm sorry. After all, we are on the
        same side. There's still a chance to save Atlanta.
        It'll be tough, but we'll come out stronger, even
        purer...

                    BRAUNSBERG
                    (confused)
        What are you talking about?

                    BOONE
                    (excited)
        Let me introduce you...

Boone runs to the door and commands its opening.

Two men in business suits walk into the room. One is
Orloff, and the other is a slick, smooth-looking execu-
tive. His name is FORREST. He extends his hand to the
President.

                    FORREST
        Good evening, Mr. President. I'm Armenyan
        Forrest, new Regional Vice President for Mikra-
        tek. And this is Master Designer Orloff from
        BlackSpear. We represent all the major corpora-
        tions in Atlanta. We've come to you because we
        need your help to save it...

EXT. "MOON QUEST" – DAY
Instead of being in Atlanta, we are on the harsh surface
of the moon. Space technology (at least in Moon Quest)

has advanced. Special nano-fiber clothing allows the characters to walk around the orb's surface without the heavy, cumbersome space suits of the past. The game DOES simulate the moon's gravity, however, so as the players move, they are forced to move almost in slow motion.

At the entrance of the moon base, the character of LUNA, a superb black-haired woman dressed in a skin-tight body suit and holding a massive laser weapon faces three SILICA WORMS.

> LUNA
> Back off, you slimy losers! The Moon Base belongs to us!

> SILICA WORM
> (hissing)
> Leave our world, Earthling! You have no place here!

Luna spits and aims her weapon.

> LUNA
> We named it, we claim it, Worm!

The Silica Worms seem to grow in size and open huge maws filled with teeth dripping slime. They slither towards Luna, hissing and roaring. It looks like the young woman has her work cut out for her.

Suddenly, an ALARM BELL rings. The battle scene FREEZES on Luna's fierce, agitated face.

INT. KOREY'S LOFT – DAY

Instead of Luna, we see Korey's face; her expression mirror's the one on the screen. The ALARM BELL is still ringing.

Korey is standing in the holo-chair. The image of a mobile phone is BLINKING in the corner of the game screen. She makes a finger gesture in the air and Morel's face appears on the screen; he looks viciously happy. Korey obviously recognizes him.

> KOREY
>
> Yeah?

> MOREL
>
> Stanton there? I need to talk to him now!

> KOREY
>
> He's asleep. I don't know what you guys do to your people... You sure it can't wait? He'll be in a shitty mood if I wake him up.

> MOREL
>
> He'll be in a worse mood if you don't wake him up, sweetheart. Boone wants to see him ASAP.

Korey, concerned, gasps at the mention of the name.

> KOREY
>
> Boone! Patrick's not in any trouble, is he?

> MOREL
>
> How would I know? No more than usual, I suppose. Now, go get his ass out of bed

KOREY

It's your funeral, Morel.

She puts him on hold. Immediately, the screen SHOWS a series of colorful commercials and jingles.

She gets out of the holo-chair, picks up a mobile phone and walks to the bedroom.

INT. BEDROOM – DAY

Stanton is asleep in the middle of a messed up bed.

Korey walks into the room, drops the phone on the bed, and shakes him.

KOREY

Get up, Pat! Wake up! Morel wants to talk to you.

Stanton wakes up. He looks tired, and very unhappy.

STANTON

What? What time is it?

KOREY

(pointing at the mobile)
Twelve. I didn't want to wake you, but Morel insisted. He says they want you at H.Q.

Now, Stanton becomes downright angry.

STANTON

What? The fucking son of a bitch! He can't do that to me. This is my day off.

He grabs the mobile and Korey leaves. Morel's face comes onto the screen.

> STANTON
>
> What the fuck is wrong with you, Morel? I work nights. You hear me, nights! If you can't keep your fucking schedule together, hire more Cops!

> MOREL
>
> Stuff it, Stanton! Boone wants to see you now.

A pause. Stanton is stunned.

> STANTON
>
> Crazy Mitch? What does he want?

> MOREL
>
> You can ask him yourself.

> STANTON
>
> Okay. I'll be down in a couple of hours...

> MOREL
>
> You'll be down now or you'll end up out of a job.
>
> (a pause)
>
> I hope you didn't have time to screw your girlfriend, asshole.

He hangs up. The screen goes dark. Stanton throws the phone onto the floor.

STANTON

Shit! I'll get you for this, Morel... if it's the last thing I do.

He starts to put on his clothes. Korey comes back, picks up the phone and watches him, concerned.

KOREY

If they let you go before six, come back. I work nights this week.

Stanton kisses her lightly then leaves.

EXT. WAREHOUSE – DAY

Stanton's car comes roaring out of the garage and onto the street.

EXT. POLICE HQ – DAY

POLICE HQ is a conglomeration of concrete blocks, fairly reminiscent of a bunker. There appears to be a great deal of activity everywhere.

INT. OFFICERS' HALL – DAY

Contrasting with the rest of Atlanta, this room is pristine, if a bit gloomy. It is painted in the sickly green commonly found in hospitals and other institutions.

Stanton is lying, relaxed, eyes closed, in a black, leather armchair, his feet on a coffee table.

Baracca is sitting, crouched, nearby, smoking one of her opiate cigarettes. Occasionally, she gives a sidelong glance at the door.

The silence is heavy. Baracca attempts to break it by making conversation.

> BARACCA
> What's keeping him? I should be on patrol by now. I'm going to lose my bonus.

> STANTON
> (eyes closed)
> Fuck your bonus! This is my day off. It's bad enough that I have to be here, without listening to you bitch about shit.

Baracca's eyes narrow. Stanton's anger triggers her suspicions. Her face takes on a wicked expression.

> BARACCA
> Yeah? So how are things going with you and Korey these days?

Stanton shoots her a "don't you dare" glance. But it would take more than that to stop Baracca at this point. She knows she has struck gold, and beams.

> BARACCA
> She kicked you out, didn't she?

> STANTON
> No! But even if she did, it'd be none of your fucking business.

BARACCA

Okay, she didn't, but I bet it was still a flop, eh, Big Man? Can't get it up anymore? You'll have to dump the bitch. She no good for you...

Stanton is not amused. He contains his anger.

STANTON

You're a fucking asshole, you know that?

Baracca laughs at his frustration.

BOONE (O.S.)

I see you're both in a good mood.

Boone has just walked into the room. He gives the two Cops a cold stare then turns more towards Stanton.

BOONE

So, you're Patrick Stanton...

Stanton turns his head but does not get up.

STANTON

Yeah.

BOONE

I heard you trashed your car last shift... in a brush with Death.

Baracca throws Stanton an "I told you so" look. Stanton seems a little uncomfortable talking about this.

STANTON

Yeah... I got a replacement; Morel was pissed.

Boone makes a gesture of dismissal.

BOONE

Don't worry about it. I just wish you'd nailed that bastard. He's been a pain in the ass for too long. Now, come with me.

They start towards the door. Suddenly, Boone stops and looks sideways at Stanton.

BOONE

By the way, I read in your file that you don't like to take off your gloves. You don't have any... problems, do you?

There is a long silence. Stanton appears calm outwardly, but tension is building in the room.

STANTON

Lots of Cops like to stay in uniform...

A couple of well-armed GUARDS enter the room.

Baracca takes a couple steps away from Stanton.

BOONE

True. But somebody that didn't know you might think that you're trying to hide some kind of Critter disease... Guana skin, scales...

A pause.

BOONE
We must all be pure, Stanton!

Stanton looks at Boone, at the guards, at Baracca who is trying very hard to look at anything but him.

Slowly, and with great emphasis, he takes off his gloves.

He waves his naked, normal-looking hands, fingers stretched, in front of Boone.

STANTON
Satisfied?

BOONE
(turning)
You can't be too careful. Follow me.

Stanton puts his gloves back on his hands. They all leave the room.

INT. POLICE HQ – OBSERVATION ROOM – DAY
A three-dimensional animated SUV is on a monitor screen.

A female OPERATOR is at work in front of the terminal.

The office is sparsely furnished. There is a metal desk, covered with graphs and blueprints, a few plastic chairs and a lamp. Behind the desk is a large, rectangular observation window. It is black, completely opaque. Next to the window is a small metallic door.

CAMERA PANS BACK to the main door, which opens. Boone enters, followed by Stanton, Baracca and the two guards.

> BOONE
> (to the Operator)
> Take five.

Silently, she nods and leaves the room.

Boone sits behind the desk. He looks distractedly at the documents spread in front of him. He pushes some papers around. Finally, he turns towards the two officers.

> BOONE
> You probably wonder why I wanted to meet with you...
> (a pause)
> You're good. Both of you. I've looked at your files, you're the best we have.

Stanton exchanges a quick, puzzled glance with Baracca, who shrugs but remains silent.

> BOONE
> (to Stanton)
> You've been patrolling Downtown...
> (to Baracca)
> And you, Midtown, right?

The two Cops nod in unison.

BOONE
(shaking his head)
What a waste. That's no job for Cops like you.
You must be bored...

STANTON
You know, as long as we're patrolling...

BOONE
Yes, of course... As long as you're patrolling. I
see...

STANTON
Listen, Chief, what's up?

BOONE
Just checking to see if you like your current as-
signments, that's all.

STANTON
An assignment's an assignment. It's our job. We
don't have to like it.

BOONE
Sure, but...

STANTON
But?

Boone gets up and walks around the desk. He fishes a
small transparent box out of his pocket and offers some
of the colored pills it contains to the two Cops.

BOONE

A push?

Stanton takes a single pill. Baracca grabs several, which she swallows all at once.

Boone pockets the box, looking pleased with himself. He takes in a deep breath.

BOONE

Okay, I'll come straight to the point. Have you heard of the Bunker?

Stanton and Baracca shake their heads to indicate that they have not, while looking like they are trying to figure out what is going on.

Boone smiles, a cold, superior kind of smile.

BOONE

Good. Very few people have. The Bunker is a top secret research facility set up by Black Spear a few years ago to study the incidence of genetic mutations that have been occurring in Atlanta and in all the other Independent Nations as well. As you can imagine, it's a hot potato. So knowledge of its existence has been "need to know."

STANTON

What does it have to do with us?

BOONE

We want you to take something there.

BARACCA

We're not mailmen! There are people paid to do that kind of thing...

Stanton, quicker to smell a rat, interrupts her.

STANTON

Where is it?

BOONE

Pueblo, Colorado.

Baracca's eyes grow wide. Stanton whistles.

STANTON

Pueblo? That means crossing most of the continent; what's left of it, anyway.

BOONE

I realize it might present a challenge, but you have to understand that this kind of research carries certain risks and not everyone...

BARACCA

We're not interested.

Stanton looks thoughtful.

STANTON

How many couriers have you lost?

Boone licks his lips and looks faintly embarrassed.

BOONE

A few, but...

STANTON

How many?

BOONE
(annoyed)
Four, maybe five... I don't know. Most of 'em
didn't even make it past Chattanooga. That's
why we've decided not to use couriers anymore.
They're not fighters, survivors... like you.
(a pause)
Think you can make it to the Bunker and back?

Baracca looks outraged.

BARACCA
Of all the dirty, crummy jobs I've...

Stanton interrupts her once again. A weird flame burns
in his eyes.

STANTON
It depends what kind of wheels we get.

Boone's eyes light up.

BOONE
A Hummer Titan. Series F. With a Robur engine.

Stanton whistles again, visibly impressed.

Baracca looks from Boone to Stanton, and back to Boone. She feels powerless to stop the events that are already in motion, and looks concerned.

Boone presses his advantage, dangling temptation in front of them.

                    BOONE
          You want to see it?

                    STANTON
                (nodding)
          Sure.

Boone presses a button. The black window LIGHTENS and becomes transparent, revealing a vast garage floor. In its center is a battletruck, steely grey, shining under the neon lights. Several WELDERS and MECHANICS are at work on it.

Stanton's eyes grow wide. He is fascinated by the giant machine.

Baracca, equally fascinated, gets closer to the window and whistles.

Boone smiles. He puts his hand on Stanton's shoulder.

                    BOONE
          Come on. We'll take a closer look...

He opens the metallic side door and exits. The others follow him.

INT. POLICE GARAGE – DAY

Boone and the two Cops walk down a flight of metal stairs. Stanton looks at the battletruck, completely entranced.

The Titan is a glorious machine. It has reinforced fenders, huge engraved tires, axle spikes, front blades and gun turrets. The light shines on the metal monolith. It looks like an evil monster, watching, ready to spring.
Stanton, ahead of the others, reaches the battletruck and caresses its chassis. Then, he turns back, looking vaguely embarrassed.

Boone has noticed Stanton's fascination. His smile grows wider.

> BOONE
> Gives you quite a jolt, eh? You'll get used to it. It's like a wild beast. You have to tame it... Understand its power before you can control it...

A pause. Boone stares at Stanton with intensity.

> BOONE
> So you'll take the job?

Baracca butts in.

> BARACCA
> Wait! Stanton and I have to talk. You can't...

BOONE

I forgot. There'll be a $100,000 bonus for the trip. Valid in all the Independent Nations. For each of you, of course.

BARACCA

A hundred grand! Fuck me!

Stanton walks back from behind the Titan. Suddenly, he no longer looks entranced, but very canny.

STANTON

You must be peeing yourself, Boone.

BOONE

What?

STANTON

Five hundred grand or no deal.

BOONE

You're crazy!

Baracca does not seem quite sure of what Stanton is trying to do, but the large amount of money mentioned is too much for her to resist.

BARACCA

Yeah. Stanton's right, we want five hundred grand. Each.

                    STANTON
          Don't feed me any shit. There are half a dozen
          Cops on the force that'd kill their own mothers
          to handle a Titan. Baker's crazy enough to pay
          YOU to do it, and he's as good as any of us...

A pause. Stanton knows he is on to something, so he
continues.

                    STANTON
          So I figure you must want us for some other rea-
          son. Something the others won't touch. Some-
          thing really dirty...

Boone stares at Stanton, hate in his eyes, but remains
silent.

                    STANTON
          What's the cargo?

                    BOONE
                (tight-lipped)
          I can't tell you. It's security. Classified.

Stanton turns and grabs Baracca who has followed the
exchange with a greedy look in her eyes.

                    STANTON
          Then, sorry, Chief, but it's no deal. Come on,
          Baracca.

                    BOONE
          Wait.

Stanton stops -- but does not turn.

                    BOONE
          I'll can your ass, Stanton. I say the word and
          you're chicken feed.

Stanton continues walking.

                    BOONE
          Okay.
                    (a pause)
          You'll be sorry. You're in too deep. You can't
          back out.

Baracca looks suddenly very worried.

                    STANTON
          Sounds fine. $500,000 and the nature of the car-
          go, and you've got yourself a team.

                    BOONE
          You really are a shit, Stanton. Okay. Come here.

The two Cops follow Boone to the back of the battletruck.

Boone pulls the doors open. Inside is a large, coffin-
shaped box, with various light indicators and cables.
BOONE

This truck has been custom-designed to carry a freeze
box. Before you go, we'll load a critter in that box and
seal it. It'll remain in a state of total sensory deprivation
during the journey. Almost catatonic, you might say.

BARACCA

A critter! You're paying us each half a mil to carry a critter?

Boone smiles an evil smile.

BOONE

This isn't just any critter. The creature that you'll be hauling is unique. A monster whose powers are lethal to all other forms of life. The ultimate plague carrier. A living instrument of death.
(he laughs humorlessly)
The perfect companion for a journey to the Bunker.

EXT. POLICE HQ – DAY

Stanton and Baracca are walking to the parking lot. Baracca looks pale and rather shaken; a situation that Stanton seems to enjoy.

BARACCA

Shit! You really got me into it, this time.

STANTON
(smiling)
I seem to recall that you were pretty excited when I raised the ante to $500,000.

BARACCA

That was before. Haven't you heard, Big Man? We're carrying the most dangerous cargo this side of the Big Blue. Even if we get back alive, they'll flush us. We're finished.

Stanton's grin grows even larger. He runs a gloved finger across his chin.

> STANTON
>
> I love it.

> BARACCA
>
> You really are crazy, Stanton.

> STANTON
>
> Smile when you say that... pardner.

Baracca spits.

> BARACCA
>
> That's the part I'm going to hate the most.

They arrive at Stanton's SUV. Stanton steps into the car.

> BARACCA
>
> Hey! Where are you going?

> STANTON
>
> (through the car window)
> I plan to eat, drink, fuck and sleep.
> (a pause)
> You know what, Baracca? I'm not afraid of this mission or our cargo. We can get the fuck outta here when it's all over and find someplace clean where we can spend all that money.

The car leaves in a hail of gravel.

<u>INT. KOREY'S LOFT – DAY</u>
Korey is hooked into the holo-chair.

<u>EXT. "MOON QUEST" – DAY</u>
Luna is driving a moon roving vehicle through a crater covered moonscape; she keeps looking over her shoulder.

Silica worms are writhing and gliding along after her; they're ugly but fast and are gaining on the motorized vehicle.

Luna's MRV hits a rock with one wheel, spins out of control and flips over, sending Luna flying through the air.

The Silica Worms spew out extra drool in their excitement to get to her.

Luna bounds on foot across the lunarscape, until she reaches a rocky mountain ridge.

She starts climbing, jumping quickly from rock to rock. The Silica Worms glide in pursuit but they are not built for climbing.

Luna laughs.

                    LUNA
        Go back to your crater and leave me in peace!

She stands there, gloriously silhouetted against the large blue marble of the Earth in the sky above.

EXT. ATLANTA STREET – DAY
Death is sitting on his bike in a dark corner of the street. The bike is idling gently.

Beneath the handlebars is master control panel, which features a small computer and keyboard.

Death types on the keyboard. We SEE the results on the screen. He inputs: "REQUEST HOLO OVERRIDE."

The screen replies: "TYPE UNIT NUMBER." Death types: "50647-29X-531."

The screen goes blank.

After a pause, the screen blinks back to life. We SEE the last shot of the previous scene -- Luna standing proudly against the sun.

SUPERIMPOSE: "ENGAGE OVERRIDE SE-QUENCE."

Death types in: "SYNC HELMET CONTROLS."

EXT. "MOON QUEST" – DAY
Luna is walking along the edge of the Lake of Dreams. Suddenly, a crevice opens beneath her feet.

She slips, almost falls into the bottomless chasm. But she manages to catch the edge of the crevice and holds herself there.

In the distance a loud GROWL shatters the silence.

Luna pulls herself up and out of the crevice. Silently, she unsheathes a mean-looking dagger from a hip scabbard.

Without warning, a giant Silica Worm slithers towards her at breathtaking speed. Luna stands firmly on her feet, ready for the attack.

Suddenly, in the blink of an eye, the worm disappears and is replaced by Death, a knife in one hand and his mace in the other.

Luna's face registers confusion. Her features FLICKER and are momentarily replaced by those of Korey. Her voice becomes Korey's.

> LUNA (KOREY)
> This isn't part of the game...

> DEATH
> But now it's a game of Death, my dear.

The whirling mace hits Luna in the shoulder. She starts to bleed, and staggers backward. She has lost all her warrior's countenance.

> LUNA (KOREY)
> This is wrong. I can't control...

She suddenly falls into the crevice, SCREAMING as she disappears into the earth.

Death stands still for a second, then blinks out of the scene.

INT. KOREY'S LOFT – DAY
Korey lies, motionless, crumpled on the floor next to the
holo-chair.

The apartment door opens silently.

Death steps inside. He walks to the chair, and pulls Korey's head up by the hair.

Korey is dead from terminal shock.

Another of Death's "pets," which had been sitting on his
master's shoulders, crawls down his arm.

                    DEATH
          She's all yours, my pretty.

The gelatinous creature nestles into Korey's hair and
onto her face.

EXT. WAREHOUSE – DAY
Stanton's car comes rushing down the street. The garage
doors open. It drives in.

INT. KOREY'S LOFT – DAY
Stanton's gloved hands punch at the elaborate lock system. We HEAR various electronic BEEPING sounds,
intercut with swear words as Stanton attempts to open
the door.

Finally, the door opens. Stanton bursts into the apartment, visibly angry. He discards his electropass.

STANTON

Korey! Why the fuck didn't you answer the door?

He walks into the living room. Instantly, he notices Korey's crumpled form, still face down next to the holo-chair

He rushes to her. He turns over her body.

Korey's face is now a grinning skull. Death's "pet" has eaten away all her facial flesh.

Stanton steps back in horror.

STANTON

Oh, God!

Suddenly, his attention is caught by a blinking light on the big screen. He looks up at it.

On the screen we READ: "YOU CAN'T PLAY GAMES WITH DEATH, STANTON. SEE YOU AT THE BUNKER."

Stanton smashes his gloved fist into the screen, which EXPLODES.

EXT. BLACKSPEAR TOWER – NIGHT
The Black Spear logo still glows in the blackness; there are several offices still lit up.

<u>INT. ORLOFF'S OFFICE – NIGHT</u>
The office is sparsely furnished, but what there is, is
high tech in style. It is dimly lit. Orloff is talking to
Boone on a computer screen.

                    ORLOFF
Did they accept?

                    BOONE
Yes.

                    ORLOFF
Good. I knew they would.

                    BOONE
I still don't understand why you wanted to trust
those two with such a delicate mission. Especially Stanton... Rotten apple, bad attitude...

                    ORLOFF
I have my reasons.
          (a pause)
The freeze box will be delivered in the morning.

                    BOONE
My men will take good care of it.

                    ORLOFF
See that they do.

He cuts the communication and remains sitting pensive-
ly in the dark office.

INT. POLICE GARAGE – DAY
The Titan sits quietly, still giving off an air of menace.
The lights switch ON and we HEAR the DEAFENING
ROAR of the engine being started.

INT. BATTLETRUCK – DAY
Stanton sits behind the wheel. His face is grim, but
clears as he starts a careful examination of the dashboard. With all of its buttons, lights and dials, it looks
like a jet.

Between his seat and that of his Copilot, a small GPS
screen emits a soft, regular BEEPING sound.

Sitting in the Copilot's seat is Baracca, who is also busy
playing with the gunner's console.

As she presses various places on the touch screen, we
SEE gun turrets rotate, spikes retract, etc...

> STANTON
> Fucking fantastic! What do you think?

> BARACCA
> It's gonna take me some time to figure all this
> out...

> STANTON
> You'll have plenty of that. We won't hit Nash-
> ville until tomorrow. Until then, it should be a
> piece of cake.

A pause. Uneasy, Baracca indicates the back of the truck
with her head.

BARACCA
Did they... load the cargo?

Stanton grins wolfishly.

STANTON
Yeah. I saw them load the fucker this morning.

BARACCA
What does it look like?

STANTON
Couldn't tell. It's wrapped in some kind of foil.

Baracca shudders.
BARACCA
I'm telling you, Big Man, this job stinks!

STANTON
Think of the five hundred grand and relax,
"pardner"!

He shifts a lever and the mighty engine ROARS back to
life. He gives it some more gas.

Outside, the mechanics step back.

STANTON
(leaning through the window)
Okay, this is it! Clear the floor, and open the
hangar.

INT. POLICE GARAGE – DAY
The Titan starts rolling slowly towards a tunnel.

INT. POLICE HQ - UNDERGROUND RAMP – DAY
The battletruck is moving briskly along an upward angled concrete ramp, lined with stark neon lights.

> BARACCA
>
> How does it handle?

> STANTON
>
> A real dream!
> >(he taps the wheel gently)
> Soft as silk. If you're nice to me, I'll let you drive.

EXT. POLICE GARAGE EXIT – DAY
This looks like the back of the POLICE HQ building. It is dirty, deserted, and the paint on the reinforced white wall is peeled off in several places.

A metal curtain rolls up automatically and the Titan comes ROARING into the street.

It turns right, gains speed and slowly disappears into the urban horizon.

CAMERA PANS TO the Presidential Tower which dominates the landscape.

INT. PRESIDENTIAL TOWER – GYM – DAY
The room is white with bright, fluorescent lights overhead. Along the walls are several pieces of equipment,

such as punching bags, etc. In the middle of the floor is a large wrestling mat.

President Braunsberg, dressed in traditional Sumo wrestler garb, is engaged in a practice match with another WRESTLER, almost as large as himself.

The two opponents face each other in a crouching position. Their bodies glisten with oil and sweat. Braunsberg looks more tired than the other wrestler.

Suddenly, they grab each other in a wrestling lock.

Braunsberg's opponent starts a sideways, weaving movement to try to unbalance the President.

Braunsberg's feet remain solidly planted on the tatami while he bends in a way which lowers his center of gravity, and causes his opponent to bear more of his weight.

The sideways movement stops. The other Sumo gathers his strength, his muscles bulging.

Braunsberg's mouth opens in a silent cry, and with an almost superhuman display of strength, he throws his opponent over onto the floor.

Braunsberg, covered in sweat, catches his breath with difficulty. The opponent gets up and bows.

SUMO
You have won. Congratulations. You are a great Sumo.

BRAUNSBERG
Yeah, yeah... I'm a great Sumo...

Braunsberg wraps himself in a white robe and walks towards the exit, limping. We SEE that he is badly shaken. Physically and morally.

BRAUNSBERG
(to himself)
Like hell! I used to be able to take on three kids like him before breakfast and barely break into a sweat.

He sits down on a mat.

The pet leopard that had been sitting quietly in a corner of the gym comes to his master. Braunsberg pets him distractedly.

BRAUNSBERG
I'm getting old, Aga...
(a pause)
I've done my share of dirt, but nothing like what those bastards in the towers are up to...
(another pause)
I don't think Atlanta's going to outlive me by much.

A YOUNG GIRL in a bikini suddenly comes running into the room.

GIRL
Mr. President! There's a call for you from Mr. Forrest!

Braunsberg swears.

> BRAUNSBERG
> I'll take it in the Steam Room.

INT. STEAM ROOM – DAY
Braunsberg enters. He lays down in a Jacuzzi, where the hot water slowly bubbles around his massive body. He reaches his hand towards a console imbedded in the edge of the tub, and pushes a button.

A screen slides up from the floor. The sleek, smooth looking face of Armenyan Forrest appears on the screen.

> FORREST
> Good morning, Mr. President. I'm sorry to interrupt your day this early. I thought you would like to know how the operation is progressing. Also, we have a small favor that we would like to request.

> BRAUNSBERG
> What kind of favor?

Forrest flashes a grin that is right out of a toothpaste commercial.

> FORREST
> Nothing much, I assure you. We've started to introduce the Acto-12 drug into the food and stimulants that the city distributes to its welfare population.

FORREST (cont'd)
Obviously, our own corporate employees and the municipal staff will not come in contact with the contaminated supplies...

A pause. Forrest hesitates an instant.

FORREST
However, in an operation of this scope, there is always a margin for a few... errors... My technicians advise me that the hallucinogenic phase will start in about twelve hours. You should order your police officers to be on alert for any disturbances.

BRAUNSBERG
You still haven't told me what you want.

FORREST
Well, my technicians also advise me that they expect about one percent of the affected population to survive the fatal effects of Acto-12 and remain violently insane. We'll need a small, elite division of your forces to "mop" them up.

Braunsberg snickers.

BRAUNSBERG
I'm sure that sick bastard Boone will be more than delighted to oblige you.

FORREST
I knew we could count on your support, Mr. President.

A pause.

> FORREST (cont'd)
> Our most recent polls show that thanks to the wonderful job that BlackSpear has done with their holo-games, eighty-seven percent of the population will approve of your using Acto-12 to clean up Atlanta. Once the critter population has been eliminated, your re-election is, as they say, in the bag.

The screen goes blank. Braunsberg closes his eyes and sinks lower into the tub. A small, idiotic grin plays on his lips.

<u>INT. FORREST'S OFFICE – DAY</u>
The office is plush in a very modern way. Through the large windows, we SEE the sprawling mass of the City.

Sitting in one of the uncomfortable-looking chairs that face Forrest's desk is Orloff, who has been a silent observer of the video conversation. Forrest turns towards him.

> FORREST
> Can we trust him?

> ORLOFF
> (after a pause)
> I'd have said yes, as long as his job was on the line. Now, I'm not so sure. He seems to become more unstable every day...

FORREST
What do you suggest we do?

ORLOFF
Have you considered the possibility that the operation might be even more successful if Braunsberg were to be assassinated... by a critter?

FORREST
Brilliant! That would create a public opinion backlash against the critters. We could nominate our own candidate... someone who would stand for racial purity and economic reform.

ORLOFF
I'll take care of the details.

He leaves the room.

EXT. I-75 – DAY
The Titan is moving at a rapid speed down I-75. There is nothing but urban blight on either side of the highway.

INT. BATTLETRUCK – DAY
A red, man-shaped BLIP starts blinking on the GPS screen. There is also a regular BEEPING noise.

BARACCA
What's that?

STANTON

How the fuck should I know? It's ahead of us, but it's too far away to bring it in on visual. I'll signal.

Stanton presses several places on the control panel. A red light starts blinking on the dashboard. An airhorn, similar to that of a semi-truck, starts to BLARE.

On the screen, the light starts to move from right to left, in a zig-zag pattern.

STANTON

The asshole is ignoring the emergency broad-cast.

A few seconds go by.

STANTON

There he is.

Through the windshield we a blue car can be seen going very fast and driving as if it's trying to prevent the Titan from passing it.

STANTON

If that Normal doesn't move his ass quick, I'm going to wipe him off the road for good.

He gives the steering wheel a sharp turn to the left.

EXT. I-75 – DAY
The battletruck swerves towards the left side of the road.

It accelerates, aiming at the space between the freeway's protective rail and the car. There appears to be barely enough space for the truck to pass.

The vehicles are moving at about 100 mph. The ROAR of the engines is deafening.

INT. BATTLETRUCK – DAY

Through the windshield it's obvious that the space between the two vehicles is narrowing as the Cop accelerates.

>   STANTON
>   I've got the bastard! The security system won't
>   let him get close enough to the rail.

Suddenly there is a RAT-A-TAT-TAT. A hail of ammunition smashes against the bullet-proof windshield of the Titan.

>   STANTON
>   Shit! The bastard's crazy. He's trying to kill us.

Baracca hits various controls.

>   BARACCA
>   Don't stop. I'll take care of him.

>   STANTON
>   (his head is turned towards Baracca)
>   What do you...?

EXT. I-75 – DAY
At road level the wheels of the Titan are closing fast on the blue car.

With a loud SNAP, spikes come out of the battletruck's right side.

As the Titan accelerates, the spikes tear into the blue car, and drag it along the road.

INT. BATTLETRUCK – DAY
There is the SHEARING noise of tearing metal.

                    STANTON
          Retract! You're gonna kill him.

                    BARACCA
          That's the idea.

She pushes a button, and there is a loud CRASHING sound outside.

Stanton downshifts, quickly. The battletruck GROANS, slows down, then stops.

EXT. I-75 – DAY
The Titan is stopped on the road.

Stanton jumps out of the truck and runs towards the wreck of the blue car, which has crashed against the right side rail. Baracca runs behind him.

The blue car is a mess. A door, a wheel and the hood are spilled on the road. The front and back of the car have been split apart. Bits of metal and plastic litter the ground.

                    BARACCA
        The Titan sure knows how to go about its business.

                    STANTON
        Help me!

He pulls the form of the DRIVER out of the remains of the car. They lay him on the side of the road.

The man is wearing a blue jumpsuit with a red "7" on it. His nose is bleeding and he has several gashes on his face. His eyes are open, but have a glassy look about them.

                    BARACCA
        That guy's from the "7" Oil Company. What the hell is he doing here?

Stanton ignores his partner's comment, and tries to talk to the injured driver.

                    STANTON
        You okay?

There is no answer. The man remains completely still.

                    BARACCA
        How is he?

STANTON

He looks okay to me, but he's totally fried...
    (to the driver)
What the fuck did you think you were doing
back there?

The driver keeps staring into space. He starts talking in a
voice that sounds drugged.

DRIVER

I bleed.

Stanton and Baracca look at each other, thoroughly confused.

DRIVER

I have blood on my face. Blood on my hands.
All my blood is flowing. Rivers of blood...

BARACCA

He's bad luck, Stanton. The djinn have taken
him. Let's go.

STANTON

We can't leave him here. Let's take him, and
drop him off at the next call box.

He bends to the driver, who keeps muttering deliriously
about blood.

STANTON

Come on. You're okay. You're not bleeding all
that much.

STANTON (cont'd)
(to Baracca)
Gimme a hand.

Baracca swears profusely, in a mixture of English and Arabic, while making a sign to ward off bad luck. Then, she helps Stanton prop up the driver.

Suddenly, the man coughs up blood and starts shrieking. Stanton and Baracca step back.

The man begins to laugh maniacally.

Stanton takes a step forward, but Baracca, visibly frightened by this display of sheer insanity, grabs her partner's arm.

BARACCA
Let's go! I tell you he's...

Suddenly the man gives a last cough, and falls.

Stanton bends down to examine the body.

The driver's face is frozen in a grimace. His mouth is bleeding profusely, and his eyes are rolled far back into his head, with only the whites showing.

STANTON
He's cooked.
(looking at Baracca with a puzzled gaze)
Just like that...

They stand motionless, silhouetted against the road.

BARACCA

It was written. Let's get out of here!

EXT. PRESIDENTIAL TOWER – DUSK

City's evening sky is reddening. The Presidential Penthouse is highlighted against the sunset.

INT. PRESIDENTIAL PENTHOUSE – DUSK

Braunsberg is lying on a huge waterbed, looking very
depressed. Boone is standing in front of him, looking
prim and proper as usual. They have obviously been involved in a conversation.

BRAUNSBERG

You're crazy. You and I are both crazy. We're
finished.

BOONE

I don't understand why...

BRAUNSBERG

No. You don't understand. You never did. You
don't understand what's happening to the world.
We're collapsing more and more every day. It's
too late, now. I feel it. It's the end...

A long pause, during which Braunsberg stares off into
the distance, as if seeing a vision.

BRAUNSBERG

Mankind was greedy. We thought we could have
everything we wanted and the Earth would always recover.

He turns and stretches his arm out towards the panoramic bay windows as if to embrace City.

BRAUNSBERG

But we were wrong. The heat is changing everything and we can't fight it anymore. It's all decaying. Even the people have been caught up in the death struggle. Man is becoming more bestial all the time. And the changes are as much of the spirit as they are of the flesh.

It is plain from Boone's expression, that he is now convinced of the President's insanity.

BOONE

Don't worry. We'll have everything back under control very soon, Mr. President.

Braunsberg laughs bitterly. He hasn't even heard the security chief's patronizing reassurances.

BRAUNSBERG

We're condemned. Nature wants to get rid of us. Atlanta will be the next to go. Soon the whole Earth will be clean again, like it was before we were here.

BOONE

You should rest, Mr. President. You're tired.

BRAUNSBERG

Tired? Atlanta is imploding! Forrest is killing over half a million people with my blessing, and you say I'm tired? You are crazy!

BRAUNSBERG (cont'd)
(eyes narrowing)
You know, I was wondering how they were going to eliminate me. But you're the only one that has personal access to me...

He gets up threateningly. His sanity is now almost entirely gone.

BRAUNSBERG
They sent you!

Boone SHOOTS him.

Braunsberg falls, his chest open. The waterbed bursts and spills an oozy, oily liquid.

Boone looks at the body and texts on his cell phone.

TWO POLICEMEN enter, dragging another corpse with them. We SEE that it is the body of a critter.

They place the corpse as if it had murdered the President.

ORLOFF (O.S.)
Well done, Boone. The media will eat it up. How is the rest of the city doing?

Orloff enters the room.

                    BOONE
A few incidents within the towers, easily con-
trolled. Outside, nobody knows. We pulled all of
our men out completely last night.

                    ORLOFF
Good. Nobody must be allowed out until your
clean up squads get rid of the bodies and whatever survivors there are.

They walk to the bay window and watch the sunset.

                    ORLOFF
For the next forty-eight hours, Atlanta is on its
own.

EXT. I-75 – NIGHT
The Titan is moving down the road. Its lights shine into
the darkness. There are very few signs of life off the
highway.

INT. BATTLETRUCK – NIGHT
Stanton is still at the wheel, his face is eerily lit by the
green light of the radar screen and dash.

Baracca's head appears in the opening, from behind the
seats.

                    BARACCA
Where are we?

                    STANTON
Almost in Chattanooga. I used to patrol out here
five years ago... before we pulled out... Atlanta
wasn't a fucking sewer, then. Critters were a
new thing. We used to feel sorry for the poor
bastards. Korey says...

He stops dead. His face breaks into a mask of sorrow,
but without tears.

Baracca looks at him surprised.

                    BARACCA
What's eating you?

                    STANTON
Death. The bastard killed Korey.

Baracca opens her mouth in shock, but remains silent.

                    STANTON
He left a message. He's waiting for us at the
Bunker.
              (a pause)
I'll make sure the fucking maniac can't kill any-
body else.

He shifts, and the truck ROARS into the night.

EXT. BLACKSPEAR TOWER – NIGHT
The illuminated Black Spear logo glows in the darkness.

INT. ORLOFF'S OFFICE – NIGHT

Orloff finishes discussing some paperwork with his secretary, an attractive, young, Hindu woman, CHANKRA.

> ORLOFF
> One last item, Chankra. You'll have to field all my calls for the next few days. I'll be out of the country. Notify Mr. Forrest that I was called to Philadelphia quite suddenly.

> CHANKRA
> Yes, Master Designer.

She leaves the room.

Orloff presses several buttons on his desk. On an imbedded screen, a series of empty corridors is visible.

He shuts off the system and goes to a bookshelf.
Silently, a portion of the wall slides open to reveal a small, personal elevator.

Orloff enters the elevator, which closes behind him.

INT. ORLOFF'S LAB – NIGHT

The elevator doors slide open. Orloff steps out.

The room looks like the inside of a giant beehive. It is bathed in blue light. The walls are covered with screens and computers.

In the center of the room, on a pedestal, under a Plexiglas dome, is a vast, holographic image of Atlanta.

Hanging from the ceiling, small cameras peer down into it. Tiny, articulated, metal pincers come out of the pedestal, and manipulate silver figurines.

The whole project conveys the unmistakable feeling of some perverted, giant game.

Orloff looks at several screens, then at the model itself.

> ORLOFF
> Braunsberg was right. What amazing perception. Forrest and the other fools are too greedy to realize it but Atlanta is done for.
> (a pause)
> The Game isn't over yet. The last act will be played at the Bunker...'

He laughs maniacally, puts his hands to his eyes and removes a pair of contact lenses.

We SEE Orloff's real eyes: green and shining with slit pupils, like a cat's. If we hadn't figured it out before, we now know that Orloff is also Death.

He then opens a wall panel and pulls out Death's red skull helmet, which he puts on.

> ORLOFF
> (quoting Poe)
> "And darkness and decay and the Red Death held illimitable dominion over all..."

One of Death's "pets" comes crawling out of a corner of the lab. Death picks it up, and sets it on his shoulder.

INT. BATTLETRUCK – NIGHT
Stanton is driving. Baracca is back in the co-pilot's seat.

> STANTON
> ...It's Snake territory. They're weird, but not particularly dangerous. There used to be a pretty decent road house where we could grab ourselves a stiff one. I don't know 'bout you, but I sure could use a drink.

> BARACCA
> Sounds good to me, Big Man.

> STANTON
Besides, I want to find out what we're likely to run into up ahead...

EXT. CHATTANOOGA – NIGHT
The Titan exits I-75 and drives into what appears to be a deserted, boarded-up restaurant/gas station. An illuminated sign with portions of several letters missing reads, "CHOO-CHOO BAR."

The battletruck stops in the parking lot, which already contains half-a-dozen mean looking vehicles that are only half visible in the darkness.

INT. BATTLETRUCK – NIGHT
Stanton puts on the security brake and pulls a card out of the ignition slot.

Baracca picks up a gun and puts it into an inside holster.

STANTON

Let's go.

They open the doors.

INT. CHOO-CHOO BAR – NIGHT

The inside of the bar is dark, lit only by dim, yellowish-green lights. In a corner of the room, on an elevated dance floor, a dozen PEOPLE are eerily moving to the sound of a THROBBING CHANT.

The words of the song are unintelligible, and in fact, the scene is reminiscent of a primitive culture involved in a cultish, semi-religious ceremony.

In the rest of the bar, other PATRONS are drinking a fluorescent liquid out of tall, thin glasses.

Black-clad WAITRESSES circulate silently through the crowd.

"Snakes" resemble normal humans, except for some scaly growths on their cheekbones and foreheads, and yellowish eyes which give them something of a reptilian look.

Some of the Snakes wear paper-maché masks, which are painted as grotesque faces, representing hate and pain. Others wear headbands with strange, alphabet designs on them.

Nobody turns their heads when the two Cops enter the room.

BARACCA
You sure as hell know how to pick a fun joint, Big Man.

STANTON
They've always been kind of odd, but this is something new.

They stop at the bar. Stanton signals to the BARTENDER, who walks over silently, as if in a trance.

STANTON
Two of whatever's coldest.

The bartender goes to get the beers.

STANTON
(to Baracca)
Snakes are very religious. They believe that the mutations are the result of their sins and...

The tune of the CHANT becomes sharper, its beat increases in pace. The two Cops turn to watch the dance floor.

The Snakes have started whipping each other with thin metal bars, keeping up their chanting the whole time.

The audience watches in silence.

The bodies of the participants begin to bleed, some profusely. One Snake falls to the floor, but nobody seems to notice.

Baracca gasps.

The bartender returns with the beers. Stanton drops a few coins on the bar.

                    BARTENDER
          We no longer accept currency.

                    STANTON
          What do you take then?

The Bartender points at the dance floor.

                    BARTENDER
     Pain.

Stanton and Baracca look at each other, not knowing what to answer.

A SNAKE, with imposing muscles, wearing one of the paper mache masks, looks over from where he is sitting, gets up and walks towards them.

The attention of the other spectators slowly turns from the dance floor and begins to focus on the two police officers.

                    SNAKE
          What do you want here?

                    STANTON
          Just a couple of beers. We've been rolling all
          day. I used to stop here a long time ago. Nice
          place.

He grins uncomfortably. The Snake looks menacing.

> SNAKE
> You cannot watch this ceremony...

A pause. The Snake continues in a more fanatic tone.

> SNAKE
> ...but you can purify yourselves by joining us in
> the Brotherhood of Pain.

Baracca makes a pass with her hand, as if to ward off the
evil spirits. Stanton points at the dance floor, where
more "performers" have fallen, while the CHANTING
and MUSIC continue.

> STANTON
> You expect us to do that!?

> SNAKE
> We expect nothing... but the day of punishment
> is upon us. Those who remain impure shall be
> destroyed.

> STANTON
> I see. Well, maybe another time.

They start walking slowly towards the door.

In the audience, a Snake coughs loudly, hiccups some
blood, and drops to the floor.

Stanton has noticed the Snake's collapse.

STANTON
(to Baracca)
See that guy in red? He just died -- like the guy
out on the road.

BARACCA
You can dissect him later. Let's just get our
asses out of here while we can.

They leave the eyes under the blank stares of the Snakes.

EXT. BLUE ISLAND BAR – NIGHT
Stanton and Baracca rapidly walk towards the Titan.

STANTON
I'm telling you, something weird is going on.
First they act even crazier than usual, then they
start coughing up blood and dropping dead. That
sure as hell ain't normal.

BARACCA
Maybe it's some kind of an epidemic...

They look at each other, the same realization crossing
their minds. They then run to the Titan.

INT. BATTLETRUCK – NIGHT
Stanton crawls from the driver's compartment into the
back of the truck. He crosses a small sleeping area that
contains a bunk and a micro-kitchen, then slides open a
metal door.

Baracca follows at his heels.

They step into the cargo section of the truck. The freezer box is sitting there, its warning lights all shining green.

> STANTON
>
> I guess it's not that.
>> (a pause)
> Let's go.

EXT. CHATTANOOGA – NIGHT
The Battletruck drives into the night.

EXT. ATLANTA STREETS – DAWN
Dawn is lighting up the city skyline with a rosy glow. The streets are completely deserted.

A dead body is lying on the sidewalk. Blood and foam are clotted around its mouth. The eyes are rolled far back into its head.

It is obvious that the cause of death is the same as that of the two victims seen by Stanton and Baracca.

INT. KOREY'S APARTMENT – DAWN
Korey's body is still lying there. Maggots have started to feed on the corpse.

The apartment is now covered by a thin layer of fungus. The only noise is the occasional electric CRACKLE of the "Luna" game.

Suddenly small flat panel TV screen in the kitchen lights up. Its digital clock reads 6 a.m. A cheery anchorwoman appears.

                    ANCHORWOMAN
        It's six o'clock, and time for GOOD MORNING
        ATLANTA!

Various commercials flash by at an almost subliminal
speed.
                    ANCHORWOMAN
              Following the tragic assassination of our be-
              loved President by critters, Security Chief Boone
              has declared martial law. More violence last
              night as...

The voice of the anchorwoman becomes indistinguisha-
ble from the ROAR of...

EXT. CABBAGETOWN – DAWN
...rapid MACHINE GUN FIRE.

An Iguana is lying on the ground, mowed down by the
gun.

An armed POLICE OFFICER is standing over the body.

Boone and a squadron of Cops are searching the devas-
tated ruins of Cabbagetown. Periodically, they come
across bodies of Iguanas, showing the obvious symptoms of death by Acto-12.

More Cops come out of one of the Apartment Blocks.

                      OFFICER
                    (to Boone)
        All clear in this Block, Sir. They're all dead.

                         BOONE
             Good. Don't leave anyone alive.

He grabs a small walkie-talkie from his belt and starts
speaking into it.

                         BOONE
             Block 15, come in. How's it going down there?

                         VOICE
             All clear, Sir. We're heading back to you now.

Boone, satisfied, clips the walkie-talkie back to his belt.

There is more MACHINE GUN FIRE in the b.g. The
noise merges into that of...

EXT. NASHVILLE – DAWN
...The Titan speeding along the deserted interstate.

INT. BATTLETRUCK – DAWN
Baracca is now driving.

Stanton is manning the gunner's console, reading a map
on a video display.

                         STANTON
             We're almost out of Nashville. We should be in
             Memphis by noon, if nothing happens. That's
             when the fun really begins.

Baracca has looked distracted throughout Stanton's mo-
nolog.

BARACCA
Wrong, Big Man! The fun starts now.

She points at the GPS screen. Two red blips have materialized.

Stanton peers into a visor.

Two "mean"-looking PICK-UP TRUCKS, one red, one white, are gaining fast on the Titan.

BARACCA
You think it's...?

STANTON
Yeah. Fucking Snakes. They must have decided we were sinners after all.

BARACCA
This time we can't cut out discreetly.

She grumbles and presses harder on the gas pedal. The truck vibrates, and literally jumps ahead.

BARACCA
Let's see what they're made of...

EXT. I-40 – DAY
The distance between the Titan and the two pick-ups increases, then remains constant.

INT. BATTLETRUCK – DAY

The speedometer's digital readout is going up rapidly. A red "ALERT" signal starts blinking under the "TEMPERATURE INDICATOR."

                    BARACCA
          I'm losing them.

                    STANTON
          Slow down! The fucking engine's overheating.

Baracca notices the light.

                    BARACCA
          Shit!

But she doesn't slow down.

EXT. BATTLETRUCK – DAY

As if to prove the truth in Stanton's remark, a column of steam erupts from under the vehicle's hood.

INT. BATTLETRUCK – DAY
                    STANTON
          Slow down! You're going to kill the fucking engine!

Baracca grudgingly, and reluctantly, obeys. The speedometer's readout goes down slightly.

EXT. I-40 – DAY

The white pick-up is once again gaining on the Titan. Its front end is decorated with an enormous metal horn resembling a spear. At the speed it is traveling, it looks like it intends to ram the Titan from the back.

INT. BATTLETRUCK – DAY
Stanton is studying the GPS screen.

> STANTON
> The bastards will be in shooting distance in 30 seconds.

He starts pushing several buttons on the console. A picture of the road behind the battletruck, with the two pursuers magnified, appears on the video screen in front of him.

> STANTON
> Let's see if these rear defense systems are everything they're cracked up to be.

More buttons. A video grid appears and superimposes itself on Stanton's screen. Squares start flashing as Stanton adjusts the sights.

EXT. BATTLETRUCK – DAY
On the huge rear fender of the Titan, compartments WHIRR open, unveiling mobile laser cannons.

EXT. I-40 – DAY
Almost instantly, the two vehicles react, instantly moving out of the way of the battletruck's line of fire.

INT. BATTLETRUCK – DAY
The same image is repeated on Stanton's video screen.

Stanton bangs his hand against the console angrily.

                    STANTON
          Shit! They must've seen the lasers. They're out
          of fucking range.
                    (a pause)
          I'll get the bastards.

He grabs a huge laser rifle and stands up on his seat. He
then opens a "sunroof" type of panel in the Titan's roof.

A burst of ROARING wind invades the cabin. The
NOISE of the road becomes deafening.

                    BARACCA
          What the hell are you doing?

Stanton does not reply. He positions himself carefully,
bracing his feet against the back of the seat, and his back
against the sunroof.

He then brings the gun into a shooting position.

INT. WHITE PICK-UP – DAY
Stanton's face and upper torso are on the Titan's roof.

The Cop adjusts his sight and fires.

A BOLT of searing fire shoots across the distance, but
misses the pick-up.

A pair of scaly hands comes INTO VIEW, shifting
gears.

<u>EXT. I-40 – DAY</u>
The white truck jumps ahead, and in a supple zigzag pattern, violently SLAMS into the back of the Titan.

The horn TEARS into the rear fender, a portion of which
falls off into the road with a SHEARING sound.

We SEE the rear lasers being crushed.

The battletruck almost goes out of control, swerving violently towards the right. The tires smoke as they
SCRAPE against the road.

<u>INT. BATTLETRUCK – DAY</u>
Baracca levels off on the gas and turns the wheel in a
desperate effort to regain control.

She finally succeeds, and the battletruck once more picks
up speed.

                    BARACCA
         How's it going up there?

Stanton is clinging to the roof.

                    STANTON
         Feels like a fucking rollercoaster.

                    BARACCA
         Glad you liked it.
                   (checking the screen)
         Shit! He's coming back.

Stanton aims the laser.

113

                    STANTON
        I see him. The bastard's gonna find out if all that
        pain pays off in the after-life!

EXT. BATTLETRUCK – DAY
Stanton shoots again.

EXT. I-40 – DAY
This time, the blast HITS the pick-up dead center.

It careens out of control. It HITS the safety rail, which
bends, but does not break. Instead, it catapults the vehicle back into the middle of the road.

Stanton fires again.

The SUV EXPLODES.

Flaming debris SCATTER across the road. The burning
skeleton of the cabin continues to roll for a small distance, before finally stopping, and CRACKLING sinis-
terly.

The dead driver is a carbonized husk.

EXT. BATTLETRUCK – DAY
Stanton has watched the explosion from the roof. He
looks grimly satisfied.

                    BARACCA (O.S.)
        You're getting pretty good, Big Man.

                    STANTON
Don't open the champagne yet. The slime in the
red pick-up hasn't made his move.

                    BARACCA (O.S.)
After what happened to the last one, ten to one,
he'll quit.

EXT. I-40 – DAY
As if to give the lie to Baracca's words, the red pick-up
starts aggressively closing in on the battletruck. There
are TWO MEN inside.

EXT. BATTLETRUCK – DAY
                    STANTON
Guess it's my lucky day.

                    BARACCA (O.S.)
Shit! What good's all that money gonna do me if
I'm dead?

Stanton raises his gun.

EXT. I-40 – DAY
The red pick-up is too quick for Stanton. Suddenly, in a
totally unexpected fashion, it brutally HITS the left side
of the Titan.

EXT. BATTLETRUCK – DAY
Stanton almost loses his balance. He clings to the roof to
prevent himself from falling onto the roadway.

Inadvertently, he drops the laser rifle, which rolls down
the roof towards the back of the truck, but gets caught on

a hanging piece of metal, which keeps it from falling into the road.

INT. BATTLETRUCK – DAY
Baracca controls the giant machine with difficulty.

EXT. BATTLETRUCK – DAY
Deciding to make a move to get his rifle back, Stanton pulls himself out of the sunroof.

INT. BATTLETRUCK – DAY
Baracca watches, horrified, as Stanton's legs slide up, then disappear from the inside of the truck.

BARACCA
Stanton! What the hell are you doing? You're crazy! Get back in here!

EXT. BATTLETRUCK – DAY
Holding to a rack that is on top of the battletruck, Stanton crawls towards where the laser is hanging.

EXT. I-40 – DAY
The red pick-up again violently slams into the Titan.

EXT. BATTLETRUCK – DAY
Stanton loses his grip, and rolls along the truck's roof. He manages to catch a hold and keep himself from falling off. He is now within grabbing range of the laser.

He rests for a second, his face reflecting his knowledge of his precarious position.

Suddenly, there are several SHOTS. Bullets whiz by the Cop; one of them grazes his sleeve.

Stanton flattens himself on the roof.

EXT. I-40 – DAY
One of the Snakes, wearing a hate/pain mask, crawls threw the pick-up's back window and stand up precariously in the truck bed. He holds a Winchester-type rifle, and he is taking shots at Stanton.

EXT. BATTLETRUCK – DAY
Stanton swears. Slowly, he grabs his rifle and crawls back towards the sunroof.

EXT. I-40 – DAY
The Snake gets back inside the pick-up.

Now free of Stanton, the red pick-up again prepares to attack. Vicious-looking blades SNAP loudly out of its right and left front bumpers.

The blades are positioned lower than the Titan's chassis. Now that the truck's rear defenses are gone, the pick-up intends to slash the truck's tires, and cause it to crash.

EXT. BATTLETRUCK – DAY
Stanton is still only halfway back inside the battletruck.

He watches the pick-up, and suddenly understands what its driver is planning.

He drops back inside.

INT. BATTLETRUCK – DAY
Stanton lands on his seat, rifle in hand. Without catching his breath, he shouts.

> STANTON
>
> Brake!

> BARACCA
>
> Brake? At this speed? You crazy.

> STANTON
>
> Brake, or the bastard will fucking slice our tires!

Baracca grips the steering wheel as if she is trying to pull it apart.

Stanton locks on his seatbelt and shouts.

> STANTON
>
> Now!

Baracca brakes.

EXT. I-40 – DAY
The Titan SCREECHES.

The red pick-up comes CRASHING into the rear of the truck with a thunderous EXPLOSION. Glass and metal fly in all directions.

It's clear that the driver didn't have time to position the blades precisely. They do nothing more than TEAR harmlessly into the metal of the Titan.

INT. BATTLETRUCK – DAY
The two Cops are seriously shaken by the crash. Several dials on the dash are shattered.

We HEAR an EXPLOSION.

Stanton punches something into the control panel.

STANTON
I'll jettison the shock absorbers.

EXT. BATTLETRUCK – DAY
A portion of the huge metal bumpers that protect the battletruck's rear, fall onto the road with a loud, metallic THUD.

Some pieces of metal, enmeshed with the burning portions of the pick-up, are still dragged along by the Titan for several feet, but finally CLATTER as they fall free.

INT. BATTLETRUCK – DAY
The two Cops are sweaty and shaken, but look happy.

STANTON
We did it! We got the fuckers!

BARACCA
Crazy Mitch isn't paying me enough for this kind of shit...

STANTON
Cut the crap. You love it.

BARACCA
Sure, it's good for my skin.

Stanton starts LAUGHING, but stops abruptly. He hears, as do we, a soft PINGING noise. He turns his head to locate the origin of the sound.

Suddenly, he jumps over the back of the seat.

STANTON
Holy shit!

He opens the door of the cargo bay.

The freezer box sits there ominously. Several lights are blinking red. Wisps of white vapor are escaping from cracks in the container.

STANTON
Shit!

BARACCA (O.S.)
What is it?

STANTON
We'll have to stop. Our little stunt's fucked up the cargo.

EXT. CHATTANOOGA – DAY
There is the rusted husk of what, at one time, must have been a station wagon. It is now invaded by swampy vegetation, and inhabited by a multitude of insects.

This is the same exit of the freeway that Stanton and Ba-racca took the previous night to go to the "Choo-Choo Bar."

There is the sound of a powerful motorcycle.

Orloff comes ROARING down the ramp. He stops near the husk, and looks around.

The "CHOO-CHOO BAR" sign looks even more miser-able in the daylight.

INT. CHOO-CHOO BAR – DAY
The floor of the bar is now littered with dead bodies, which melt into an amorphous mass in the greenish light of the room. Some Snakes are sitting motionless at their tables.

Orloff enters. His glowing green eyes shine softly in the dark. He surveys the place, then walks towards one of the sitting Snakes.

Under his boots, we HEAR a CRUNCHING noise, as he walks over the bodies on the floor.

Orloff extends his arm to touch one of the Snakes, but as he does so, the body falls to the floor, dead.

Orloff bends to examine it. We RECOGNIZE the same symptoms of death, caused by the drug, Acto-12.

Suddenly, we HEAR a SHRILL scream.

Two powerful hands push out of the sea of bodies and grapple Orloff to the floor. However, Orloff manages to roll away and get up.

A heavily-built SNAKE, wearing no mask, stands up, blocking Orloff's path out of the bar. His skin is covered with yellow, viscous sweat, and his eyes burn with an insane flame.

The two men are standing face to face in the greenish, body-littered, landscape of the bar.

SNAKE
You betrayed us, Death!

Orloff remains silent. His two, glowing eyes shine more brightly.

SNAKE
You gave us the Faith...

ORLOFF
Foolish Snake. Death does not give -- he takes away.

Snarling, the Snake lunges at Orloff, who nimbly avoids him.

Then, in a quick series of moves, Orloff pulls out his mace and a short whip, which ends in two razor-sharp blades. He starts using the latter to keep the Snake at bay.

The steady WHISTLING sound seems to panic the Snake.

                    ORLOFF
                (almost gently)
        Come, Snake. Join your friends in death.

The Snake takes a few steps backwards, then suddenly, he spits.

The yellowish liquid misses Orloff by inches, and instead splashes onto his "pet," which had been sitting on his shoulder.

The creature drops to the ground, HISSING and SCREECHING in agony.

The creature's flesh dissolves under the attack of the Snake's venom.

Orloff watches the small creature, as if in silent sorrow. He then turns towards the Snake. For the first time we HEAR a tinge of anger in his voice.

                    ORLOFF
        You will pay for that, Snake. Your time has
        come. Embrace the arms of Death.

Suddenly, another image of Orloff seems to step out of the original. Then, another and another.

In the span of a heartbeat, there are four identical Orloffs, all standing there.

The Snake now looks cornered, panicked.

He spits again, but his venom goes harmlessly through one of Orloff's phantom images.

From the expression on his face, we realize that he now knows he has lost, and almost welcomes his end.

Orloff's whip comes clawing into the Snake's neck, pulling him forward.

With a swift BLOW of his mace, Orloff breaks the Snake's skull, then lets the body fall to the floor with a THUD.

Orloff then pushes a hidden button in his glove, and his holographic images disappear.

He turns to survey the rest of the bar. His attention comes to rest on the counter.

Lying on it is the money left earlier by Stanton.

Orloff walks over to the counter and picks up the money. He then laughs softly.

                    ORLOFF
          The Bunker...

EXT. MEMPHIS – DAY
A huge sign, covered by tropical moss reads, "WELCOME TO MEMPHIS." We are at the outer edges of City.

Memphis at one time appears to have been a riverside metropolis. Now it has been reclaimed by jungle and swamps. Parts of the interstate have collapsed. The atmosphere is hot and muggy.

The Titan is stopped in the middle of a large plaza that is still relatively free of vegetation.

EXT. BATTLETRUCK – DAY
One of the truck's back doors is open. The other was crushed during the battle.

Stanton and Baracca are arguing, pointing at the freezer box, which is now leaking vapor from several places.

BARACCA
You can't let that... that thing out of the box.

STANTON
What the fuck else can I do?

BARACCA
Why don't you just ignore it and go on to the Bunker? It's their problem, not ours.

STANTON
No way! If we don't open the fucking box soon, it'll die. I won't let it.

BARACCA
Shit! It's not our fault if we got hit. They'll understand. We get paid the same either way.
(a pause)
If you open that box, we're gonna die. I know it.

STANTON
Why do say that?

BARACCA
I don't know.
        (a pause)
Boone said it was lethal.

Stanton slaps his hand against the truck.

STANTON
I don't believe a word that fucking, lying bastard said...
        (a pause)
I'm opening it.

He enters the truck.

INT. BATTLETRUCK – DAY
Stanton has grabbed a crowbar and smashes several mechanisms on the sides of the freezer.

Baracca looks on from outside the truck.

Having succeeded, Stanton, breathing heavily, lifts and pushes aside the top cover of the box.

It falls to the floor with a CLANG. More white vapor rises from the box.

STANTON
Oh, Shit!

BARACCA

What? What?

She jumps into the truck and looks inside the box. Then, she gasps.

STANTON
(softly)
Luna.

CAMERA PULLS UP to reveal the inside of the box and its occupant, Luna.

The beautiful, black-haired girl is lying naked inside the box. Her eyes are open wide, but, unlike those of her "game" persona, they are yellow and cat-like. Her lips have been sewn together with copper-colored wire.

Luna wears an expression of mute appeal. She looks very beautiful... and very tragic.

EXT. BLACKSPEAR TOWER – DAY
The sun is pounding mercilessly on the towers of City, which stand proudly over the now-deserted streets.

The BlackSpear Tower stands above it all. Then, we begin to HEAR an ALARM BELL.

INT. BLACKSPEAR TOWER – DAY
The alarm bell CLATTERS.

Three COPS rush along a mall of shops. People watch in surprise as they pass.

They arrive at a plaza where several dozen people have gathered. They disperse most of the crowd.

Two figures stand in the center of the mob. One is a heavy black man (CORONA), dressed in an expensive-looking business suit, and wearing a pair of flesh-like gloves.

The other, a SMALLER MAN, is lying on the floor, wiping blood from his face, and clutching at his chest. He is dressed in a worker's overall.

> POLICE SERGEANT
> What's going on here?

The large executive looks at him imperiously.

> CORONA
> Arrest this man. He attacked me. I'm Vice President Corona of BlackSpear.

The Police Sergeant looks at the smaller man suspiciously. He doesn't look very threatening, and seems to have a couple of broken ribs after his encounter with Corona. He looks more like a victim than a mugger.

Then, the Sergeant takes a good look at Corona, whose appearance is that of power and respectability. He quickly makes up his mind, and, with a nod to the other two Cops, orders the arrest of the small man.

> POLICE SERGEANT
> Book him.

The two Cops lift the small man, who winces in pain, and carry him away.

Before they disappear, the man turns his head and coughs up some blood.

> SMALL MAN
> (weakly)
> Ask him... His hands...

He then passes out.

Corona looks around him, apparently satisfied. The scene is back to normal.

> CORONA
> Thank you for your help. You can go now.

He turns as if to leave. This annoys the Police Sergeant.

> POLICE SERGEANT
> Wait a minute. I decide who can go... and when. Why did that man attack you?

> CORONA
> Do we have to do this now? There are a hundred thousand workers awaiting my decisions. Every minute I waste here with you costs us a small fortune.

> POLICE SERGEANT
> (uncertain)
> I need to report the incident...

Sensing victory, Corona presses his advantage.

                    CORONA
          What happens in BlackSpear Tower is Black-
          Spear's business alone. We will notify the prop-
          er authorities. Now, I'm leaving.

The big man's display of power has the opposite effect
from what he wanted. The Police Sergeant's expression
hardens and he pulls out his gun.

                    POLICE SERGEANT
          Don't move.

Corona's eyes blaze at the effrontery of the Police Sergeant.

                    CORONA
          Are you insane? You'll pay for this, Officer.

                    POLICE SERGEANT
          Show me your hands.

Corona blinks in surprise at the man's audacity. The Cop
seems surer of himself now.

                    CORONA
          What?

                    POLICE SERGEANT
          I'm asking you to show me your hands. Is that
          clear enough for you?

Corona runs his tongue over his lips. He looks at the gun pointed at him then pulls off his gloves.

He presents the back of his hands to the Police Sergeant. They look normal.

> CORONA
> (sarcastically)
> Are you satisfied? May I go now?

The Police Sergeant studies Corona's hands. From his expression, he could be contemplating the rapid dismissal from the Force that he has brought upon himself. He feels cornered, and this gives him an inspiration.

As Corona starts to put his gloves back on, the Police Sergeant interrupts.

> POLICE SERGEANT
> Wait!

The big man stops.

> POLICE SERGEANT
> Turn them over.

Suddenly, Corona turns his hands palms towards the Police Sergeant and jumps at him SCREAMING.

In the center of his palms, are quivering suction cups making an obscene SLURPING noise.

Corona succeeds in putting his right palm on the left side of the Police Sergeant's face. The Cop SCREAMS.

The two men fall to the floor, grappling, in a concerto of ANIMAL-LIKE NOISES.

The Police Sergeant manages to gain the upper hand, and shoots Corona, who collapses onto the floor.

The hand separates from the Police Sergeant's face with a sickening TEARING sound.

The Police Sergeant looks in horror at the body lying at his feet. CLOSE UP on his face, the left side of which is a raw wound.

People have started to gather. Several SCREAMS are heard.

The alarm bell RINGS again.

EXT. MEMPHIS – DAY
It is the middle of the afternoon. The heat is oppressive. The Titan sits on the Plaza.

EXT. BATTLETRUCK – DAY
Baracca wipes the sweat off her face. She is walking next to the truck with Stanton. She takes a deep breath.

BARACCA
Why are we still here?

STANTON
I need to know...

132

BARACCA

Need to know what?

STANTON

What they plan to do to her at the fucking Bunker! That's what!

Baracca shakes her head sadly.

BARACCA

I don't understand you. It's none of our business.

STANTON

I fucking want to know.

BARACCA

Shit! Why do you care? She's just another critter. It's just another job.

Stanton doesn't answer. His eyes look out into the distance, and there is a dreamy look about them.

STANTON

Nothing seems to make sense anymore. I should be in bed with Korey. We'd be fucking each other's brains out...
            (a pause)
I'm tired. I don't want to be responsible for another person being crushed by those bastards in the towers...
            (more firmly)
If they're going to hurt her, I won't take her to the Bunker.

133

Baracca looks at him with astonishment.

> BARACCA
> I don't fucking believe it!

Stanton refuses to look at her, and says nothing. Baracca explodes in anger.

> BARACCA
> Listen, Big Man! I'll go on a recon' to give you time to think about this. But I want you to know something; I haven't made this trip for nothing. I'm being paid to deliver a cargo, and I'll deliver it. With you or without you!

She turns and walks away.

<u>INT. BATTLETRUCK – DAY</u>
Stanton climbs into the truck.

Luna is now lying on a hastily arranged couch, wrapped in a blanket. She moves weakly, as the effect of the freeze box slowly wears off.

Stanton crouches to be at her level.

> STANTON
> How are you feeling?

Luna nods "yes."

> STANTON
> We don't want to hurt you.

Again, she nods "yes."

Stanton points to the row of metal wires that hold Luna's lips sewn together.

>   STANTON
>   I have something in the tool kit that I can use to
>   cut those wires.

Luna reacts with terror. She shakes her head to indicate "no" repeatedly, while putting her hands in front of her face. Stanton looks puzzled.

>   STANTON
>   You don't want me to take off the wires?

Luna shakes her head "no."

>   STANTON
>   Why?

Luna makes a series of gestures, but the Cop doesn't understand.

Seeing this, she starts tracing letters in the dust on the truck's floor.

Her finger is drawing "P," "O," "I," "S..."

>   STANTON
>   Poison! You mean there's poison in those wires?

Luna nods affirmatively.

STANTON

Shit! Who's the fucking bastard who did this? Boone?

She shakes her head "no."

STANTON

The President's henchmen?

She shakes her head "no" again, and starts drawing.

On the truck's floor she has drawn the simple figure of a skull.

STANTON

Death! That fucking pile of shit! When I'm through with him...

Luna points at her mouth and writes again.

Stanton bends and reads.

STANTON

"Pull -- don't cut" Pull?

He bends closer to look at Luna's mouth.

Her lips appear to be sealed by one single metal wire that makes half a dozen vertical slashes through her face and over her lips. One can see the end of the wire coming out of her face, just beneath, and to the left of her mouth.

STANTON
Pull the wire... but it's going to hurt like hell!
And, if it breaks you're going to...
(firmly)
No. I can't.

Luna pushes her face forward in an unmistakable plea.
Stanton thinks for a second then gives in.

He walks wordlessly towards the drivers' compartment,
and comes back with what looks like a first-aid kit. He
smiles apologetically.

STANTON
A little anesthetic. It may help some.

Then he pulls off his gloves and flexes his hands as if
getting them accustomed to the feel of the air.

Stanton's hands move to Luna's mouth and begin to
gently tug at the wire. Luna winces. Some blood starts to
trickle from the wound.

The wire comes out of the first hole. Stanton continues
to pull at the next hole. And the next.

Luna's face contorts under the pain, in spite of the anesthetic. The bottom of her face is washed with blood.
Stanton's is concentrating intensely.

EXT. MEMPHIS CONDO – DAY
Baracca is standing on top of a building that was once a
condo complex. The concrete is now cracked by the

tropical vegetation. There are pools of dirty water on the roof.

She surveys the area. In the direction that they're heading, there is a sea of green vegetation, broken by an occasional building.

Behind her in the direction of Atlanta, huge clouds are gathering. In an almost subliminal flash, we see the clouds turn red and waver. A low RUMBLING is heard. The picture is heavy with a sense of doom.

Baracca shakes her head, and enters the building.

EXT. MEMPHIS STREET – DAY
Baracca walks out of the condo, and into the street. Various reptiles scatter out of her path.

She turns into a larger street that leads to the Plaza where the battletruck is parked.

EXT. BATTLETRUCK – DAY
Baracca, with large strides, crosses the Plaza and heads towards the Titan.

Stanton and Luna are waiting for her. Luna's lips are now covered with a thin, silver plastic film.

                    BARACCA
          (coldly)
     So?

                    STANTON
     We go.

138

> BARACCA

We go?

> STANTON

We go. There's a lot to tell you. We can do that on the road.

They all get into the truck. We HEAR the noise of the engine being started.

The Titan shakes then slowly moves across the Plaza. It disappears into one of the swamp-filled avenues of Memphis.

INT. BATTLETRUCK – DAY

Stanton is driving. Baracca is at the gunner's console. Luna sits in the middle. A heavy, uncomfortable silence permeates the cabin.

> BARACCA

I'm waiting.

Stanton points at Luna.

> STANTON

Death did that to her... He's a real shit. His real name is Orloff. You never met the bastard, but I did. He's a bigwig at BlackSpear, a game designer. He's crazy. Absolutely fucking crazy! It's like all those years of building games pushed him over. He doesn't see the difference between games and reality anymore. Atlanta and all that's left of the South ... are like his own personal chess board -- and we're all his pawns.

BARACCA
I don't understand. Where do we all fit into that?

Stanton gives a short, bitter laugh.

STANTON
We're Orloff's own, personally selected toys.
Just like from under a fucking Christmas tree.
Luna's the prize and we're the players.

Luna speaks with great difficulty.

LUNA
No... Bunker...

STANTON
There is no fucking Bunker. He made it all up.
The crazy bastard's waiting for us. He's waiting
to kill us down the road.

More thunder RUMBLES in the distance.

EXT. MEMPHIS – EVENING
Orloff, on his motorcycle, slowly rolls into Memphis.
Night is starting to fall, but he seems to have no inten-
tion of stopping.

EXT. BATTLETRUCK – EVENING
The Titan rolls out of the swampy streets, into a crum-
bling shopping center. The vast, glass windows have
long since been shattered. The truck drives into one of
the buildings and stops.

INT. MEMPHIS SHOPPING CENTER – EVENING
The driver's door opens, and Stanton jumps out, quickly
followed by Luna.

> STANTON
> We'd better stop here. We can't go any further
> tonight.
> > (a pause)
> We can try to find a way across the Mississippi
> tomorrow.

Baracca comes around the front of the truck. Her confidence, which until now had been unshaken, shows signs
of faltering. In the failing light, she suddenly looks much
younger and less self-assured.

> BARACCA
> Why don't we turn back?

Stanton is taking provisions and equipment from the
truck and lays it on the ground.

> STANTON
> No. We're going to see this through to the end...
> > (he taps his gun)
> Besides, by now there probably isn't much of
> Atlanta left to go back to.

Baracca looks at him without understanding. Stanton sits
down next to the equipment, and starts to prepare a meal
out of their scanty provisions.

STANTON

Luna told me about more than Orloff. Remem-
ber all those people that we saw die on the way
out here? They were poisoned. The bastards put
some kind of drug into the water to kill off the
critters. They think that's going to save Atlanta.

Baracca's eyes go wide in horror.

BARACCA

But that means killing over half a million
people! They can't do that!

Stanton nods grimly.

STANTON

They can... and they are.

Luna moves over, next to Stanton. She still speaks with
difficulty, but it seems somewhat easier now.

LUNA

It won't work. Atlanta is dead. Orloff knew it.

BARACCA

(at Stanton)

What does she mean?

STANTON

That's why Orloff wanted her out of the way.
She's special. She can sense the future, and
she's seen Atlanta burning, just like when Sher-
man marched to the sea.

EXT. MIKRATEK TOWER – NIGHT
Standing tall against the dark, deserted streets of City,
Mikratek Tower has an ominous air. The penthouse
window is lit up.

INT. FORREST'S OFFICE – NIGHT
Forrest is pacing the room, looking upset.

Boone is sitting in one of the chairs, looking harassed.
He is wearing dark glasses, which completely cover his
eyes.

> FORREST
> This is not going the way we planned it. My
> board is going to be upset by this news.

> BOONE
> We're making progress in regaining control of
> BlackSpear's lower levels.

Forrest throws his arms up in the air, walks towards his
desk, and angrily grabs a stack of reports.

> FORREST
> Regaining control? Ha! Look at these reports.
> It's getting worse.

He starts reading reports.

> FORREST
> Riots OTP and ITP. Critters turning up, even in
> the executive suites. 52,000 deaths caused by
> Acto-12 -- in my own tower...

                    BOONE
        An error in the...

Forrest starts to panic.

                    FORREST
        Shut up! You're involved in this as much as we
        are. I don't care how you do it, but you and
        those incompetents that work for you better get
        this mess cleaned up.

Boone stands up and wordlessly leaves the room.

Forrest goes to his desk and pulls out a new bottle of
pills. He breaks the seal, pours himself a glass of water,
and swallows a couple.

EXT. MEMPHIS – NIGHT
The silence of the night is broken by eerie sounding animal CRIES. The street is deserted; a covered manhole is
visible.

There is grunting, then a pair of clawed hands slowly
push the manhole cover aside with a RUSTY SQUEAK.

A misshapen figure climbs out of the hole, and melts
into the night.

INT. MEMPHIS SHOPPING CENTER – NIGHT
Stanton is standing guard by a small fire.

Baracca gets out of the truck, and lights up one of her
thin brown cigarettes. She takes a few puffs.

                    144

STANTON

How is she?

BARACCA

Sleeping.
                    (a pause)
You like her, eh, Big Man?

STANTON

Yeah. I guess I do.

There's a long pause.

BARACCA

Do you believe her? That the city is done for?

STANTON

I think I've known it for awhile. But, there were just too many things keeping me there. Korey, memories of Atlanta the way it used to be... when we all thought we could have a better future...

BARACCA

What are we going to do now?

STANTON

I don't know. Tomorrow is the end of the road. Death is waiting. After that, who knows?

Baracca takes a few steps outside of the shopping center. In the far horizon, in the direction of Atlanta, comes a sound like the RUMBLING of a storm. She shivers, and goes back inside.

<u>EXT. MEMPHIS SHOPPING CENTER – NIGHT</u>
The misshapen figure, skulking in the darkness, notices the light of Stanton's fire.

Moving stealthily, it enters the building.

In the sky above, a lightning bolt ERUPTS. The storm breaks and a sheet of water cascades from the sky.

<u>INT. MEMPHIS SHOPPING CENTER – NIGHT</u>
Stanton and Baracca move closer to the broken window to watch the rainstorm.

Suddenly, there is a RUSTLING noise.

Stanton turns and searches the darkness. He sees nothing and returns to watching the storm.

>STANTON
>It should clear by morning.

>BARACCA
>(to herself)
>Water for the dead.

>STANTON
>What?

>BARACCA
>In my country, that kind of rain, they call it "water for the dead."

The storm rages on.

EXT. MIKRATEK TOWER – NIGHT

The storm is striking the tower with an almost sentient fury.

INT. FORREST'S OFFICE – NIGHT

The bottle of pills is now lying shattered on the floor. Forrest's dead body is contorted nearby.

His face shows the symptoms of death by Acto-12.

EXT. MEMPHIS – DAWN

The sun breaks through the last remnants of the clouds. It looks like it's going to be another hot day.

The streets are flooded. The vegetation shines a luxuriant green. Mosquitoes and flies buzz everywhere.

Suddenly, one of the older buildings collapses with a CRASH. The weight of the water and vegetation has destroyed it. A flock of birds flies away with terrified SQUAWKS.

INT. MEMPHIS SHOPPING CENTER – DAWN

Stanton is lying on the floor, next to the battletruck, asleep. He awakens with a jump at the sound of the CRASH.

Baracca comes out of the driver's cabin.

> BARACCA
> What was that?

Stanton has already gone to the window to take a look.

> STANTON

House went down. Stress and age, I guess. Some of these places weren't that strong to begin with.

Baracca looks outside with a pensive expression on her face.

Stanton grabs his utility belt, and walks towards the truck.

> STANTON

Let's get going.

He climbs into the Titan.

INT. BATTLETRUCK – DAY
The couch on which Luna was lying is now empty.

INT. MEMPHIS SHOPPING CENTER – DAY
Stanton jumps out of the truck.

> STANTON

Luna! She's gone!

> BARACCA

Lemme see.

She gets into the truck.

INT. BATTLETRUCK – DAY
Baracca is crouched near the empty couch. Stanton is standing outside the rear of the truck.

Baracca points at footprints on the dusty floor.

BARACCA

She sure didn't walk out of here alone...

STANTON

Orloff?

BARACCA

No. No boots. Most likely a Crawler.

STANTON

We have a problem...

INT. MEMPHIS SEWERS – DAY
The two Cops are hip deep in a rushing flow of dirty, debris-filled water. They are progressing slowly, guns in hand.

They are in an underground tunnel, large enough for half a dozen people. Some light comes from street level grids, which also add more water to the tunnel. The grey concrete walls are covered in fungus.

BARACCA

I hate sewers!

STANTON

Crawlers live in sewers. There's a good chance that the one that took Luna has his nest around here somewhere.

The two Cops reach an intersection.

BARACCA

What do we do now?

STANTON
(pointing)
I guess we have to split up. You take that one.

BARACCA
O.K., Big Man. I'll meet you back at the truck at
ten hundred.

She walks into the tunnel.

INT. MEMPHIS SEWERS – A DIFFERENT SECTION – DAY

The tunnel is smaller here, and the flow of liquid is more
viscous. Once in a while, a fetid-looking bubble bursts
on the water's surface.

From the expression on Baracca's face, we can tell that
the odor, too, has worsened.

The tunnel makes a sharp right turn. Baracca walks
slowly and with extreme caution.

Suddenly, she notices a large hole in the wall. It appears
to have been dug after the sewer.

From the hole we SEE a crude, dirt-walled tunnel going
off into the distance.

She examines the hole and her hand closes on the bones
of several small animals.

BARACCA
Crawlers...

She climbs into the hole, where she can only move forward on her hands and knees.

She continues to keep her gun at the ready.

INT. CRAWLERS' NEST – DAY
Baracca comes out of the hole into a large, square room that must be the cellar of one of the buildings above.
It is filled with boxes, torn pieces of cloth, putrefying food, etc. On the floor are a dozen bodies, completely still.

BARACCA
Oh shit!

She goes to one of the bodies, and turns it over for closer examination. The corpse is covered with hair, and has a rat-like appearance. Its death was obviously caused by Acto-12.

Baracca stands up and walks slowly through the room, looking at the other corpses. She starts shivering. Her face reflects a gnawing fear.

Suddenly, Orloff's BOOMING voice fills the cellar.

ORLOFF (O.S.)
Alexandria Baracca!

Baracca turns sharply. In the same movement she SHOOTS at Orloff, who is standing at the far end of the room.

Her bullet passes harmlessly through one of Orloff's holographic images, and SLAMS into the wall.

Another image of Orloff appears in a different part of the room. The green glow of his eyes shines evilly in the darkness.

ORLOFF
Officer Baracca, you are face to face with Death. Prepare yourself for your final battle.

Orloff raises his arm above his head and begins to revolve his bladed whip.

Baracca looks wary. She takes a few steps backwards, and squints at her enemy. We SEE Orloff waver slightly, as if he is another of the holographic images.

Baracca notices the wavering.

BARACCA
Are you too frightened to do your fighting in person, like a man?

Orloff laughs.

Suddenly, the bladed end of the whip comes WHISTLING out of the darkness. It is real, and it SLASHES Baracca's arm, making her drop her gun.

The Cop jumps backward to avoid the next deadly blow.

BARACCA
(panting)
You're not a hologram!

ORLOFF
Death has many tricks.

Orloff succeeds in STRIKING Baracca again.

The Cop falls to the floor. She scurries away, trying to hide behind the various crates.

Orloff again laughs softly. With one blow of his mace, he SHATTERS the crates behind which Baracca is hiding.

The Cop has had time to catch her breath. She grabs her service knife, and silently crawls out of the way.

Orloff now stands in the center of the room, looking for her.

ORLOFF
You should know better, Officer. You can't hide from Death.

Baracca lies sweating, trying to hide amongst the corpses. She hopes that her enemy will come within reach of her knife.

There is a long moment of silence, as each opponent tries to outwait the other.

Finally, Orloff makes his move. He walks towards the place where Baracca is lying.

As he comes closer, the Cop jumps and STABS him in the shoulder. With one hand gripping his neck, she prepares to stab him again.

Orloff drops his whip, and in a nimble movement, lifts the Cop over his head, and sends her SPRAWLING to the floor.

He then grabs his mace, and attempts to smash her head, but Baracca rolls out of the way.

The opponents are now standing face to face, moving round like dancers.

> ORLOFF
> You play the game well, Baracca.

Baracca looks grim, but doesn't answer.

> ORLOFF
> Did you talk to Luna, Officer? Did she tell you your fate?

Baracca's eyes enlarge slightly. We HEAR her off screen voice as she remembers her warning to Stanton.

> BARACCA (V.O.)
> "If you open that box, we're gonna die. I know it."

Orloff senses that he has struck a sensitive nerve, and moves to exploit it.

> ORLOFF
> Your fate is to die here, Baracca. Here, at Death's hand. Embrace your destiny.

> BARACCA
> Noooo!

Leaping, she jumps on Orloff, striking with her knife. Both fighters SPRAWL to the floor, and for a few seconds, we see only their bodies, tumbling and GRUNTING.

Suddenly, we SEE Orloff's arm coming up with a knife and SLASHING downward.

We HEAR a CRY.

Then, Orloff stands up and looks down at Baracca's bloodied body.

> ORLOFF
> Death conquers all.

Limping and clutching his shoulder, he disappears into the darkness.

INT. MEMPHIS SEWERS – YET ANOTHER SECTION – DAY
Stanton is carefully searching his section of the sewer. He enters ever more narrow tunnels.

Suddenly, the shape of the CRAWLER jumps on him and sends him SPRAWLING into the water.

A fight ensues, during which each opponent in turn gains the advantage.

Eventually, Stanton, the stronger of the two, manages to wear out the Crawler.

He then drags the dazed creature to its feet.

Stanton slams the Crawler against the wall, and starts questioning him.

> STANTON
> Where's Luna?

> CRAWLER
> The woman? I did her no harm...

As if to prove him right, Luna climbs out of the hole. Stanton relaxes visibly, but continues to question the Crawler.

> STANTON
> Why did you take her?

> CRAWLER
> All my family is dead. You Normals poisoned them. I saw you come here, so I took her... Then I saw him.

> STANTON
> Who?

                    CRAWLER
              (afraid)
The evil one. His face was like a skull. His eyes
glowed...

Stanton reacts in shock.

                    STANTON
Death? You saw Death? Where?

                    CRAWLER
In our nest. He came and...

Stanton grabs Luna's arm and runs in the direction from
which he came.

                    STANTON
      Baracca!

EXT. MEMPHIS SHOPPING CENTER – DAY
Stanton climbs out of the manhole and then lifts Luna
out. He rushes towards the Titan, which we can SEE inside the shopping center.

INT. MEMPHIS SHOPPING CENTER – DAY
Stanton comes running into the shopping center, but
stops abruptly. Luna, who is following, catches up with
him. An expression of horror is painted over their two
faces.

Lying propped up against the Titan is Baracca's battle-
torn body.

Luna puts her hand on Stanton's shoulder. Her voice is now back to normal.

LUNA
He's waiting for you. At the Bunker.

In spite of his obvious grief, Stanton replies.

STANTON
But, you said there was no Bunker...

LUNA
For us, no. But I see inside his mind. He's mad, and for him, it exists. He's waiting there now.

EXT. ATLANTA – DAY
Several of the towers appear to have been heavily damaged by fires and rioting. Many of the windows are shattered, etc. We HEAR the noise of EXPLOSIONS and GUNSHOTS.

BlackSpear Tower looms above everything else.

INT. BLACKSPEAR TOWER – DAY
Boone and a squadron of COPS are being besieged by a mob, in what looks like a wrecked shopping mall. It's littered with bodies. Most of the mob appears to be critters.

Boone, in tattered uniform, but still wearing his dark glasses, orders his men.

BOONE
Kill! Kill them all!

A group of combatants climbs over the barricade erected by the Cops, and attempt to rush Boone's men. However, they are quickly slaughtered by the Cops' superior force.

Suddenly, a piece of metal thrown by a member of the mob hits Boone in the face. His glasses fall to the floor. SCREAMING, he puts his hands to his eyes.

Surprised, several Cops turn around.

> OFFICER
>
> Are you hurt, Sir?

> BOONE
> (weakly)
>
> No... no...

> OFFICER
>
> Let me see...

Before Boone has time to protest, the Cop walks to him and pulls his hand from his face. The man immediately drops Boone's hand and stares in horror.

His eyes have become all black with facets, like an insect's.

The Officer gasps, and instinctively grabs his gun. The other Cops stop fighting and stare wordlessly.

Boone reaches out with his hand, as if to stop him. The policeman reacts with fury.

OFFICER
Die, you filthy monster!

He shoots Boone.

Meanwhile, the mob has grown more daring. They rush the demoralized Cops. The police soon disappear under a mass of bodies.

EXT. MISSISSIPPI RIVER – DAY
The muddy waters of the mighty Mississippi lap at the banks. The river is now huge; it is impossible to see one side from the other.

The river front buildings and piers share the decrepit, swampy look of the rest of Memphis. The atmosphere is redolent with the feeling of a thriving place that is now diseased and useless.

Strangely, the decay stops at the riverbank, where the water has touched. The river is a new frontier, as it was in the days of the Pioneers and somehow seems to be a force of purification.

A fishing boat is tied to one of the piers. Perhaps because of the river's purifying effects, it appears to be in better shape than the rest of the man- made objects near the bank.

Stanton and Luna are walking along the river. The Titan is behind them, parked on one of the desolated piers.

Luna looks more ethereal than ever as she looks out at the beauty of the river. A light breeze ruffles her hair.

Stanton looks sad and contemplative, like a man who has finally come to terms with a decision made long ago.

> STANTON
> This was always the best part of the South. It was our past and our future.

> LUNA
> My mother used to bring me here every summer... Until they said it was "unfit for human contact."

> STANTON
> Bull. Look at it.

> LUNA
> But it was! Now that the people have left, Nature has reclaimed her own. Tranquility and health have returned...

Suddenly, a bloodied knife -- Baracca's -- imbeds itself in the ground with a THUD.

Stanton jumps back, startled but not really surprised.

> ORLOFF (O.S.)
> Very well put, my dear. I always knew you were one of our best sensitives.

Orloff has appeared on the pier, his approach so silent that they did not hear him. Although he still wears

Death's leathers, he is no longer wearing his red skull helmet.

Stanton gasps as he stares at Orloff's cat-like eyes.

> ORLOFF
> Yes, these are really my eyes...
>> (a pause)
> I, too, have started to revert to bestiality...

Suddenly, an idea strikes Stanton. He looks quickly at Luna's face, with its yellow, cat-like eyes that are so much like Orloff's.

Luna, who has been staring at Orloff with a look of disgust and hate, nods sadly. She answers the unvoiced question.

> LUNA
> Yes. He's my father.

Stanton stares at the two of them, not sure what to think or do.

Orloff ignores Luna, and concentrates his attention on Stanton.

> ORLOFF
> That fool Boone was right about you, Stanton. You are the best. And, unlike all the others, you have not mutated. You remain pure...
>> (a pause)
> We were fated to meet here for the final match in my ultimate game. May the better man win.

Orloff pulls out the knife he used to kill Baracca. Stanton pulls his own service knife out of his boot.

The two men begin to circle each other warily. Orloff is limping. One of his arms has been injured in his fight with Baracca. Stanton is wearied by the rigors of the trip and his encounter with the Crawler.

Orloff is the first to strike. He lashes out with his knife, but Stanton manages to leap out of the way, unscathed.

Several more attacks follow, all avoided by Stanton.

The Cop carefully studies his opponent. Orloff's technique is superior to his, but Stanton is stronger.

Orloff feints an attack and, switching hands in a flash, lunges at Stanton. This time, the policeman is almost caught by the knife, but he manages to avoid the deadly blow.

The two fighters, PANTING, warily watch each other. Orloff GROWLS softly, like a tiger.

> ORLOFF
> It's better this way. A victory that comes too easily is meaningless. But don't get your hopes up, Officer. Death always wins in the end.

Stanton doesn't reply. He is saving his energy for the fight.

Luna stands behind the two men. Her eyes are closed and she has an almost peaceful expression on her face, as if she already knows the outcome of the battle.

Orloff lunges at Stanton again, and projects his leg forward, intending to kick the policeman in the chest.

Stanton rolls to the ground to avoid the blow, and quickly regains his feet as Orloff lunges at him once again.

This time, Orloff is off balance from his parry, and Stanton's knife SLICES into his arm. Orloff GROWLS again, sounding even more animalistic.

Both Stanton and Orloff are now showing great fatigue. They are breathing heavily, and their faces are covered in perspiration.

Stanton decides to pursue his advantage. He launches a quick series of blows against his opponent. Orloff backs up, losing ground.

Suddenly, he pulls a second knife, seemingly out of nowhere, and lashes at Stanton.

The Cop tries to escape the blow. This time, however, he is not quite fast enough, and he too is wounded, in the chest. He starts to bleed.

Another pause follows.

Knowing that he must make a move soon or lose, Stanton launches himself at Orloff. Both men grapple.

Orloff tries to stab one of his knives into Stanton, but the policeman's superior strength sends Orloff SPRAWL-ING to the ground.

One of his knives escapes his hand. Stanton kicks it aside.

Orloff watches as Stanton, standing over him, hesitates for a microsecond, deciding whether he should kill his enemy now that he is down.

The madman GROWLS yet again, and presses on his glove.

Suddenly, there are two Orloffs, both getting up and coming at Stanton with their knives.

Then, a third one appears.

Stanton is confused. He starts moving back. Then, he makes a desperate decision, and launches himself at the Orloff to his right.

Luna, her eyes still closed, suddenly shouts.

LUNA
No, Patrick! Not that one! You must attack the one on the left!

Without pausing, Stanton changes his direction. His left hand comes up to block the real Orloff's blade which was about to enter his neck.

Thrown off guard by Stanton's move, Orloff leaves his side unprotected for a second. Almost immediately, Stanton plunges his own blade into Orloff's chest.

With a look of surprise in his eyes, and the soundless word "no" on his lips, Orloff FALLS to the ground, dead.

Stanton stands there, eyes closed, his head bowed in exhaustion.

He then straightens up, walks to Orloff and pulls his knife free.

He stands for a moment and looks at the dead man, his face showing no emotion at all. He then turns and walks over to where Luna is waiting.

                    STANTON
          Thanks.

Luna looks up at him. Her face, too, is emotionless.

                    LUNA
          He was right in a way. Your meeting was fated...
          But you were always meant to win...
                    (a pause)
          With Orloff's death, it really is over. His control
          over our lives dies with him.

They turn in the direction of Atlanta and the South.

Large columns of smoke, and occasional flames, rise above the horizon. There are many EXPLOSIONS.

Nearer to them, some of the buildings at the edge of the Mississippi River COLLAPSE like the building next to the Mall.

At the very edge of our perception, somewhere in the reborn jungle, we HALF-SEE dark, animal-like shapes, darting through the trees and the remains of the buildings. Birds CRY in the b.g.

Stanton and Luna walk towards the boat. He tentatively puts his arm to her back, as if asking her permission.

She smiles at him gently, and solidly pulls his arm around her.

They reach the boat and look at it silently for a minute.

Then, Luna gets into it.

Stanton uses his knife to cut the rope that holds it to the pier. The boat starts to float away.

Stanton jumps on board. He looks down at the deck, uneasily.

> STANTON
> I hope this thing makes it to the other side.

> LUNA
> (with certainty)
> It will.

The sun shines down on them, the boat and the pure, flowing water.

The boat gets farther and farther away, growing smaller and smaller, until it is only a dot on the horizon.

Back on the pier, next to the cut rope, lays a pair of abandoned black-leather gloves.

FADE OUT

THE END

ABOUT THE AUTHORS

Writers **Randy & Jean-Marc LOFFICIER** have co-authored five screenplays, a dozen books and numerous comic books and translations. They have collaborated on a number of animation teleplays, including episodes of *Duck Tales* and *The Real Ghostbusters* and written such popular characters as *Superman* and *Doctor Strange*. In 1999, in recognition of their distinguished career as comic book writers, editors and translators, they were presented with the Inkpot award for Outstanding Achievement in Comic Arts. Randy is a member of the Writers Guild of America, West and Mystery Writers of America.

SF & FANTASY

Henri Allorge. *The Great Cataclysm*
Guy d'Armen. *Doc Ardan: The City of Gold and Lepers*
G.-J. Arnaud. *The Ice Company*
Cyprien Bérard. *The Vampire Lord Ruthwen*
Aloysius Bertrand. *Gaspard de la Nuit*
Richard Bessière. *The Gardens of the Apocalypse*
Albert Bleunard. *Ever Smaller*
Félix Bodin. *The Novel of the Future*
Alphonse Brown. *City of Glass*
André Caroff. *The Terror of Madame Atomos; Miss Atomos; The
Return of Madame Atomos; The Mistake of Madame Atomos*
Félicien Champsaur. *The Human Arrow*
Didier de Chousy. *Ignis*
Captain Danrit. *Undersea Odyssey*
C. I. Defontenay. *Star (Psi Cassiopeia)*
Charles Derennes. *The People of the Pole*
Georges Dodds (anthologist). *The Missing Link*
Harry Dickson. *The Heir of Dracula*
Jules Dornay. *Lord Ruthven Begins*
Alfred Driou. *The Adventures of a Parisian Aeronaut*
Sâr Dubnotal *vs. Jack the Ripper*
Alexandre Dumas. *The Return of Lord Ruthven*
Renée Dunan. *Baal*
J.-C. Dunyach. *The Night Orchid; The Thieves of Silence*
Henri Duvernois. *The Man Who Found Himself*
Achille Eyraud. *Voyage to Venus*
Henri Falk. *The Age of Lead*
Paul Féval. *Anne of the Isles; Knightshade; Revenants, Vampire City;
The Vampire Countess; The Wandering Jew's Daughter*
Paul Féval, *fils. Felifax, the Tiger-Man*
Charles de Fieux. *Lamékis*
Arnould Galopin. *Doctor Omega; Doctor Omega & The Shadowmen*
G.L. Gick. *Harry Dickson and the Werewolf of Rutherford Grange*
Edmond Haraucourt. *Illusions of Immortality*
Nathalie Henneberg. *The Green Gods*
V. Hugo, P. Foucher & P. Meurice. *The Hunchback of Notre-Dame*
Michel Jeury. *Chronolysis*
Octave Joncquel & Théo Varlet. *The Martian Epic*

Gustave Kahn. *The Tale of Gold and Silence*
Gérard Klein. *The Mote in Time's Eye*
Jean de La Hire. *Enter the Nyctalope; The Nyctalope on Mars; The Nyctalope vs. Lucifer; The Nyctalope Steps In*
Etienne-Léon de Lamothe-Langon. *The Virgin Vampire*
André Laurie. *Spiridon*
Gabriel de Lautrec. *The Vengeance of the Oval Portrait*
Georges Le Faure & Henri de Graffigny. *The Extraordinary Adventures of a Russian Scientist Across the Solar System* (2 vols.)
Gustave Le Rouge. *The Vampires of Mars*
Jules Lermina. *Mysteryville; Panic in Paris; To-Ho and the Gold Destroyers; The Secret of Zippelius*
Jean-Marc & Randy Lofficier. *Edgar Allan Poe on Mars; The Katrina Protocol; Pacifica; Robonocchio; Tales of the Shadowmen 1-8*
Xavier Mauméjean. *The League of Heroes*
José Moselli. *Illa's End*
John-Antoine Nau. *Enemy Force*
Marie Nizet. *Captain Vampire*
C. Nodier, A. Beraud & Toussaint-Merle. *Frankenstein*
Henri de Parville. *An Inhabitant of the Planet Mars*
Gaston de Pawlowski. *Journey to the Land of the 4th Dimension*
Georges Pellerin. *The World in 2000 Years*
J. Polidori, C. Nodier, E. Scribe. *Lord Ruthven the Vampire*
P.-A. Ponson du Terrail. *The Vampire and the Devil's Son*
Maurice Renard. *The Blue Peril; Doctor Lerne; The Doctored Man; A Man Among the Microbes; The Master of Light*
Jean Richepin. *The Wing*
Albert Robida. *The Adventures of Saturnin Farandoul; The Clock of the Centuries; Chalet in the Sky*
J.-H. Rosny Aîné. *Helgvor of the Blue River; The Givreuse Enigma; The Mysterious Force; The Navigators of Space; Vamireh; The World of the Variants; The Young Vampire*
Marcel Rouff. *Journey to the Inverted World*
Han Ryner. *The Superhumans*
Brian Stableford. *The New Faust at the Tragicomique; The Empire of the Necromancers (The Shadow of Frankenstein; Frankenstein and the Vampire Countess; Frankenstein in London); Sherlock Holmes & The Vampires of Eternity; The Stones of Camelot; The Wayward Muse.* (anthologist) *The Germans on Venus; News from the Moon; The Supreme Progress; The World Above the World; Nemoville*
Jacques Spitz. *The Eye of Purgatory*

Kurt Steiner. *Ortog*
Eugène Thébault. *Radio-Terror*
C.-F. Tiphaigne de La Roche. *Amilec*
Théo Varlet. *The Xenobiotic Invasion*
Paul Vibert. *The Mysterious Fluid*
Villiers de l'Isle-Adam. *The Scaffold; The Vampire Soul*
Philippe Ward. *Artahe*
Philippe Ward & Sylvie Miller. *The Song of Montségur*

MYSTERIES & THRILLERS

M. Allain & P. Souvestre. *The Daughter of Fantômas*
A. Anicet-Bourgeois, Lucien Dabril. *Rocambole*
A. Bisson & G. Livet. *Nick Carter vs. Fantômas*
V. Darlay & H. de Gorsse. *Lupin vs. Holmes: The Stage Play*
Paul Féval. *Gentlemen of the Night; John Devil; The Black Coats ('Salem Street; The Invisible Weapon; The Parisian Jungle; The Companions of the Treasure; Heart of Steel; The Cadet Gang; The Sword-Swallower)*
Emile Gaboriau. *Monsieur Lecoq*
Steve Leadley. *Sherlock Holmes: The Circle of Blood*
Maurice Leblanc. *Arsène Lupin vs. Countess Cagliostro; Lupin vs. Holmes (The Blonde Phantom; The Hollow Needle)*
Gaston Leroux. *Chéri-Bibi; The Phantom of the Opera; Rouletabille & the Mystery of the Yellow Room*
Richard Marsh. *The Complete Adventures of Judith Lee*
William Patrick Maynard. *The Terror of Fu Manchu*
Frank J. Morlock. *Sherlock Holmes: The Grand Horizontals; Sherlock Holmes vs Jack the Ripper*
P. de Wattyne & Y. Walter. *Sherlock Holmes vs. Fantômas*
David White. *Fantômas in America*

SCREENPLAYS

Mike Baron. *The Iron Triangle*
Emma Bull & Will Shetterly. *Nightspeeder; War for the Oaks*
Gerry Conway & Roy Thomas. *Doc Dynamo*
Steve Englehart. *Majorca*
James Hudnall. *The Devastator*
Jean-Marc & Randy Lofficier. *Royal Flush*
J.-M. & R. Lofficier & Marc Agapit. *Despair*

J.-M. & R. Lofficier & Joël Houssin. *City*
Andrew Paquette. *Peripheral Vision*
R. Thomas, J. Hendler & L. Sprague de Camp. *Rivers of Time*

NON-FICTION
Stephen R. Bissette. *Blur 1-5. Green Mountain Cinema 1*
Win Scott Eckert. *Crossovers* (2 vols.)
Jean-Marc & Randy Lofficier. *Shadowmen* (2 vols.)
Randy Lofficier. *Over Here*

HEXAGON COMICS
Franco Frescura & Luciano Bernasconi. *Wampus*
Franco Frescura & Giorgio Trevisan. *CLASH*
L. Bernasconi, J.-M. Lofficier & Juan Roncagliolo Berger. *Phenix*
Claude Legrand, J.-M. Lofficier & L. Bernasconi. *Kabur*
Franco Oneta. *Zembla*
L. Buffolente, Lofficier & J.-J. Dzialowski. *Strangers: Homicron*
Danilo Grossi. *Strangers: Jaydee*
Claude Legrand & Luciano Bernasconi. *Strangers: Starlock*

ART BOOKS
Jean-Pierre Normand. *Science Fiction Illustrations*
Raven Okeefe. *Raven's L'il Critters*
Randy Lofficier & Raven OKeefe. *If Your Possum Go Daylight...*
Daniele Serra. *Illusions*